CONTENTS

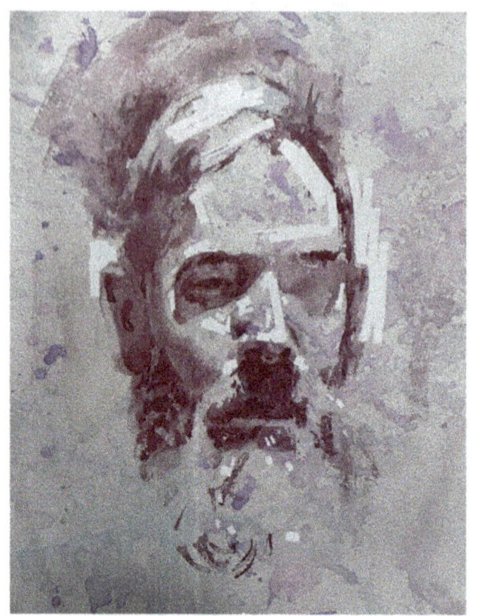

JOSEPH CHRISTY

Joseph B. Christy is a Nashville artist. Most of his life has been spent in the greater Nashville area. In addition to a degree in art from Lipscomb University, Joseph also obtained Master's Degrees in Education and Painting, from Georgetown College and Marshal University, respectively. A former public school art teacher, Joseph now spends his time raising a feral child with his wife, writing fiction, painting, and making comics. Since 2020, Joseph has been making indie comics. He has many graphic novels and multiple volumes surrounding a sci-fi kung fu sect of monks, a shared universe set in a future post civilization earth, think mad max but without the guzzoleen, that has three loosely connected tales, a couple children's books, and some one-shots. Joseph has also had multiple painting shows in the last ten years, his most recent a two man show with Matt Christy, his brother, And the horse you rode in on, at The Browsing Room Gallery. The paintings consisted of three pieces the brothers collaborated on and a handful that they didn't. The Brothers Christy have made comics together and even self-published a crime noir novel that they wrote together.

STEPHEN L. FOX

Stephen glides through life with his heart on his sleeve and thoughts three inches past his mouth. He started life as an aspiring comic artist; inspired by folks like Todd McFarlane, Wendy and Richard Pini, John Bryne, and Alan Davis.

Life marches on, though, and after a few emotional black eyes, Stephen has decided to opress friends and strangers through the written word. While his writing is often as uncomfortably personal as his dinner conversation, he's at least got a good(ish)

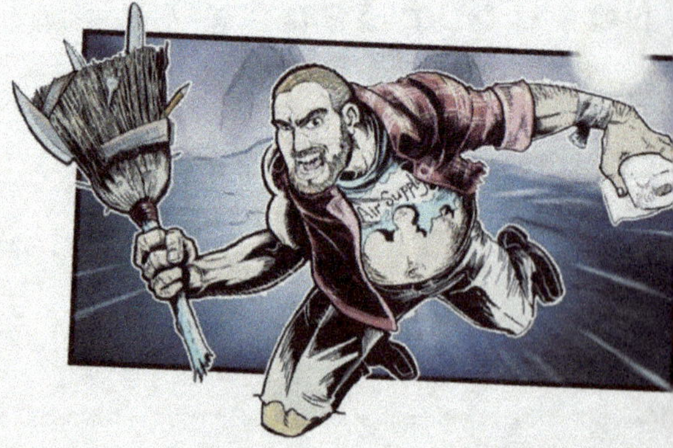

sense of humor and takes deprication from self and others with a smile or sob – depending on the Lexapro currently swiming around his skull. Stephen's never been the gallery sort (not that there's anything wrong with that), but he has worked on roleplaying games, coloring books, comics, and novella-length storybooks.

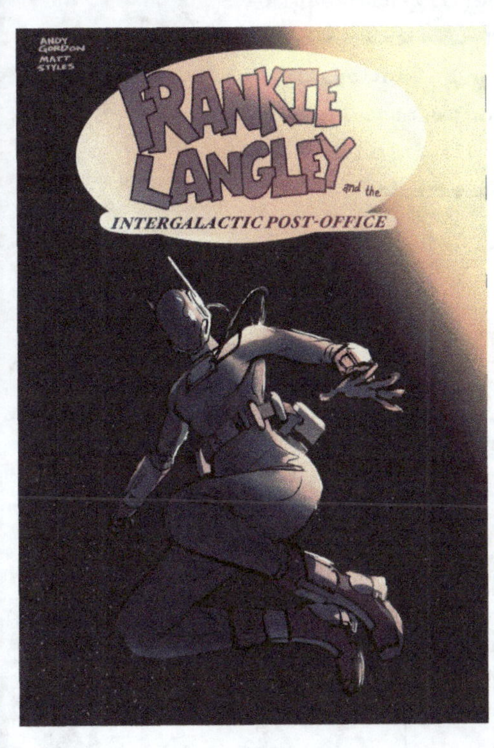

FRANKIE LANGLEY

AND THE INTERGALACTIC POST OFFICE

By Andy Gordon and

"A stubborn and crotchety mail carrier who is forced to take on a naive traì`nee so she can retire from the perilous and indifferent Inter-Galactic post office...and the two might just become friends along the way."

Keep up with the project on Andy Gordon's Instagram:

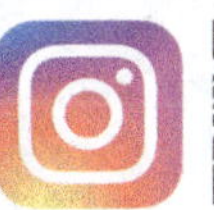 

Pickup Andy's other work on Big Cartel:
https://andygordonart.bigcartel.com/

KICKSTARTER FUNDING THIS WINTER

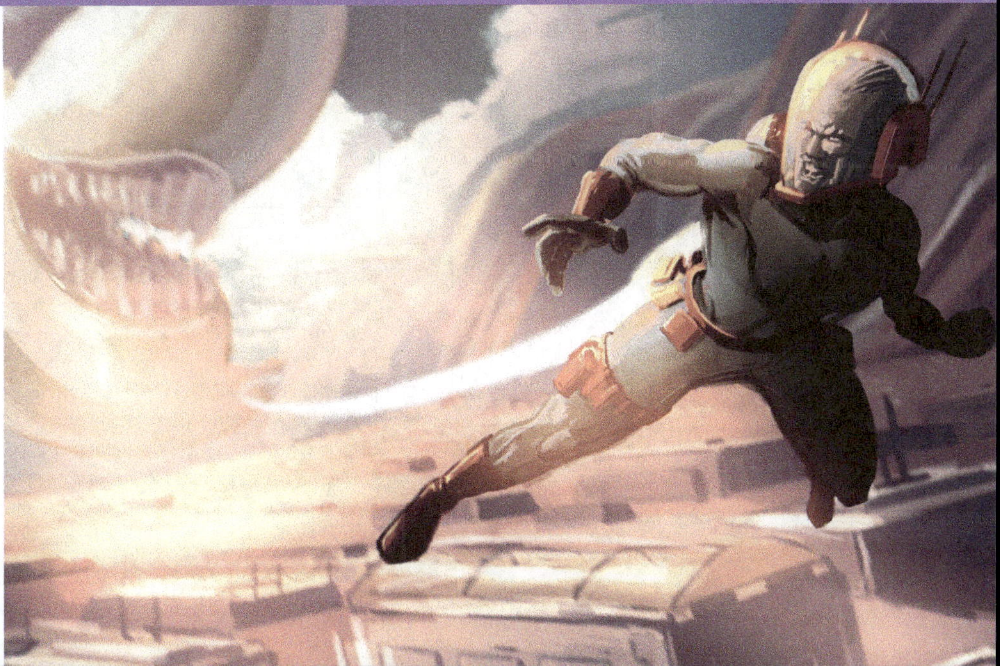

STEVE'S RANT

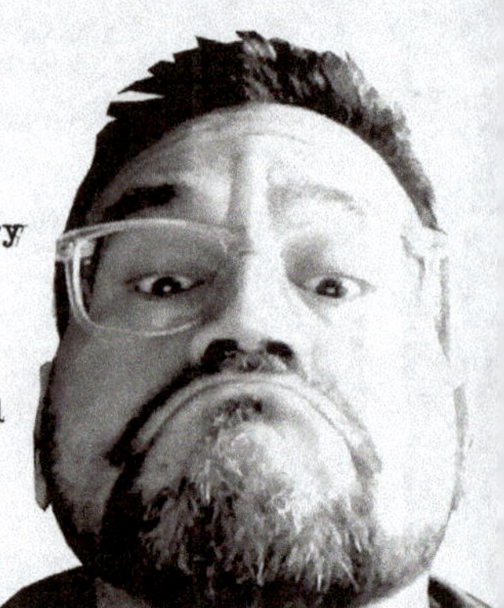

INESCAPABLE HYPOCRACY

By Stephen L. Fox

Man, I love dogs. A controversial perspective, I know. I'm all about big, bold proclamations, though. Here's another one – **indie creators are hypocrites.**

Aren't we? I mean, I spend so much time ranting about the theft of children's' icons by billion-dollar toy licensees masquerading as entertainment conglomerates. At least, that's what I'm doing when I'm not logging into Disney+ chasing inevitable heartbreak around the latest Star Wars misinterpretation. Et tú Ezra?

Sometimes I wonder if I'd be happier without any of the world's giant machines that facilitate my twenty-first century life. Fuck Amazon and their anti-union, anti-small-business footprints. Who the hell needs another Disney/Marvel movie plotted on the back of an executive's Whole Foods receipt? Kroger and their price-gouging ass can kiss *my* a – oh man, that's a really good price for chicken. Besides, my neighborhood butcher almost never asks me how my old back injury is doing anymore ...

Even this super-independent 'zine passed through Adobe's Creative Cloud InDesign©, on an Apple MacBook™, while I drank my Starbucks Venti Iced Brown Sugar Oatmilk Blonde Espresso©, and will be printed through Ingram Spark (probably the least well known behemoth on this list, but still a multi-billion dollar, soul-crushing corporation). Pardon me, my Apple Watch just pinged me to stand up.

Is it ironic that the tools of independent creators lie in the definitely-not-people companies that rule the world – Is being a hypocrite something to be ashamed of? Should my love of dogs manifest into a day-to-day respect for all sentient life which motivates me toward veganism? Maybe.

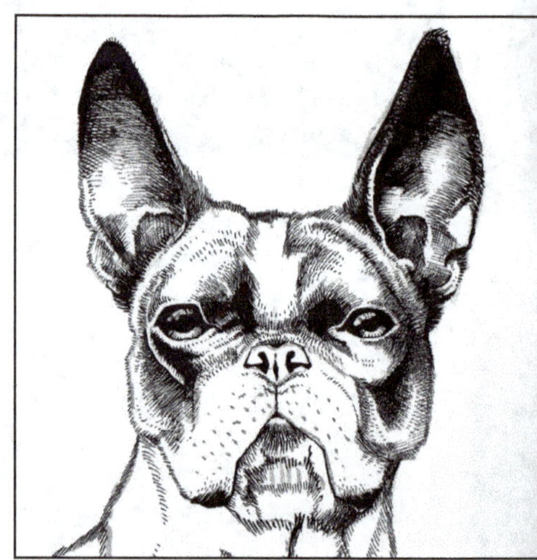

Maybe not. Maybe hypocrite is just another word for person. Maybe that conviction that makes you spout your mouth off like some Dunning Kruger moron is a bit more aspirational than practical – or even possible. While it's easy for independent creators to congregate around companies that enshroud every decision around a 12%+ annual profit, there's another cause nearly all artists I know enthusiastically engage in: like gnats around apple-cider vinegar.

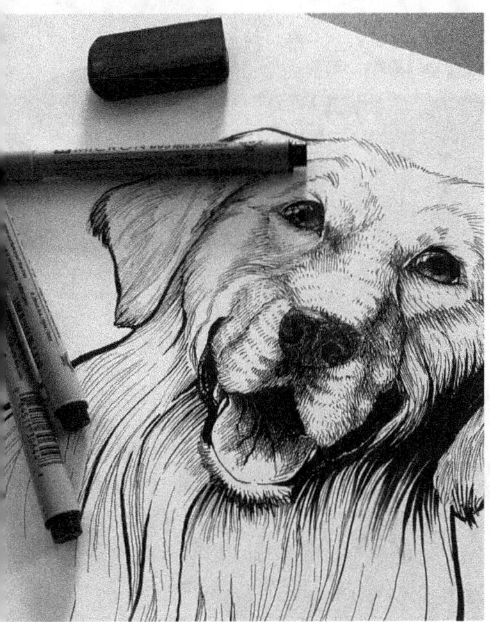

e beat the ever-loving fuck ut of ourselves.

ost artists don't obsess over the shackles corporate merica has quietly slid around our as-productive-as-ossible wrists. We do obsess over our own short-comings. e tell ourselves logical lies that fill the gaps between our assion and success. This dance we do trying to produce omething sincere **and** marketable feels so easy until it's ne to sell the damn thing we compromised our own tastes create.

hrases like "No pressure," "Sorry to bother you," "If you on't mind," and a million other disclaimer-style preempts our language about the things we make. We stand ehind over-priced convention booths with drawings of ings we didn't create hoping to catch the eyes of folks ho are there to see Kevin Eastman or J. Shawn Alexander oth fine folks (although Eastman's con fees are stupid-gh (what's up with that, Kev'?))).

he curse of independent creators is the contradiction etween our desire to say something sincere while ccumulating enough patrons to financially support us oing the sincere thing. In our minds we say art is for an udience while sometimes resenting the world for being illingly addicted to spoon-fed least-common-denominator orytelling. When we venture too far toward strategy, our eative fuel depletes and sometimes depression overtakes.

Self-flagellation begins.

"I'm not making enough."
"My stuff is too weird."
"I've sacrificed so much – why can't I just give it up?"
"Why am I so fucked up?"

But the art tick isn't one that can be twisted or burned away. It's more than who we are – it's validation of a sort none of us can properly articulate. It's too special – too enthralling, too much. We're restless without it, and even past the idea of god(s) – believe we're destined to create. We convince ourselves we're cursed – success isn't unlikely, it's impossible. Damn it. Damn them. Damn me.

I go through this cycle constantly. I'm grateful to be on the sun-side of it at the moment. I know I'll be back in the black, though. It's inevitable. My only hope lies somewhere between, and mixed with, the sadness that fuels me and the curiosity that motivates me. The thing I want most for people who see what I've done is a bit of a smile, a soft gasp, a recognition of shared experience, a moment of magical discovery. I just want to move you.

I get it, though. Smiles and gasps don't allow the pragmatic parts of life to move or improve. Doing what we love for a living is a wonderful dream – one most of us share. Is it a foolish dream, though? Maybe.

Maybe not. That's where I think a community comes in. Truth be told, who knows how long ND Riot will go. This may be the one-and-only, but I hope not. This is a second nonpaying job for many of us, and others of us are equally overwhelmed raising kids or doing any number of other physical, mental, and emotional tasks all day long. Sometimes we're manifesting creations from fumes. We need some damn grace.

We don't do that for ourselves. So, I'm asking us all to remember that other artists, and the very best patrons, want you to be well before they expect their next smile or gasp.

You're enough. Give yourself a damn break – you fucking **hypocrite.**

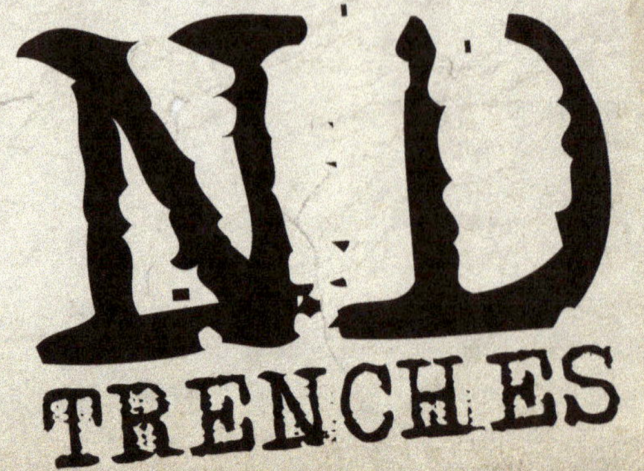

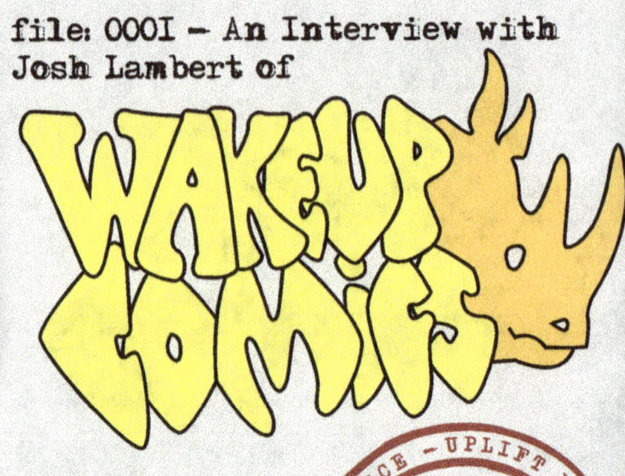

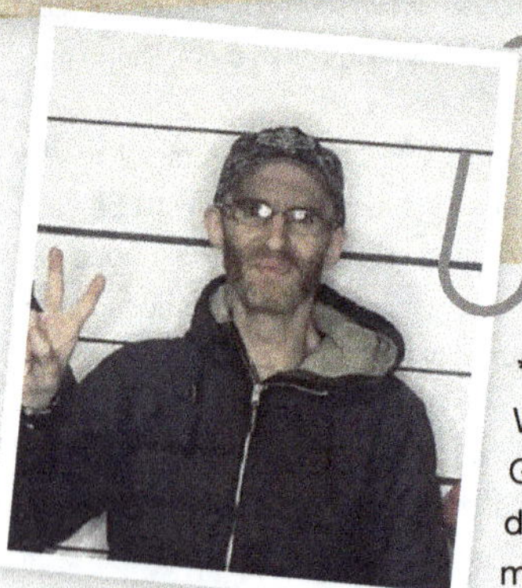

Person of Interest:
Josh "On The Lam"
Lambert

*What is WAKEUP COMICS?

Wakeup Comics is a micro-business. It's a few shelves inside The Groove, a record shop in East Nashville, Tennessee, where I sell predominantly independent and self published comics and zines. Well, mostly that… occasionally any weird printed stuff I find that is focused on comics.

*WHO IS WAKEUP COMICS?

Me, myself, and….. I'm the owner, founder, CEO, CFO… all those titles. It's just me. I'm a one man army. I mean, The Groove actually process the sales and stuff. I'm not there. I don't sit at the register or anything. That's all part of the micro business model. It's setup as consignment for sales tax purposes, so they're definitely a huge part of this since they allow me to set up there and remit those for me. But I'm the one that handles all the ordering, processing, and everything like that.

*HOW DID THIS HAPPEN? GOT A COOL ORIGIN STORY?

I was bitten by a radioactive independent comic book. Ha, the full story is there used to be another indie comic store here in The Groove called BrainFreeze Comics…I always plug this place. It existed for years before Wakeup. Anyways, it was run by Stewart Copeland, and it started in 2014 and I discovered it not long after I moved to Nashville by total happenstance. I'd never been in The Groove, I had a friend who was here visiting, a big vinyl guy, and so we went in there and I just randomly saw all these comics that I had only seen on the Internet. I'd never seen them in person. I never thought would unless I was in Chicago or somewhere, you know a bigger city, but here was BrainFreeze. He eventually moved it another location, but he kept

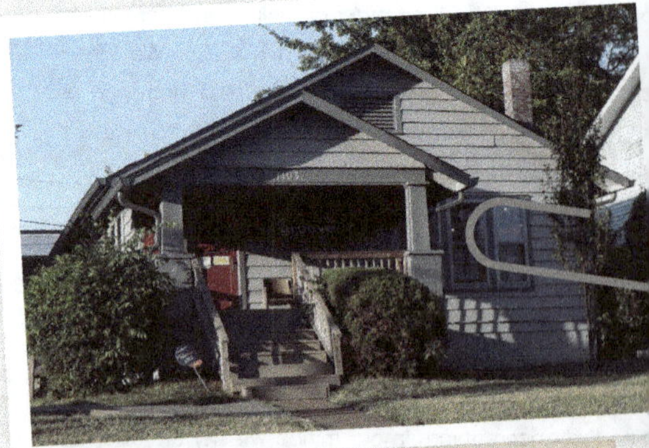

The Grove — Record store and home to Wakeup Comics
(Nashville, TN)

going for about four years and because of several factors he moved away. It shut down in 2018 and I was really disappointed. I really liked the place. And I thought it was so cool. He had that business model, and allowed him to kind of do what he did because he was not having to worry about making money off the store. So I tried to see about buying BrainFreeze, and I wasn't the only one… I think there were several people interested, but he decided not to sell it. He'd gotten rid of inventory and just kind of put it to bed. And that was that.

we got it up and running. Our shelf, now two, of indie comics and zines.

But the idea just won't let me go. I thought about it for months. So later, like still early 2018, I thought: I can just do what he was doing. Just make it my own thing. And that was kind of wierd starting up…but I decided, you know, I was gonna do it because I wanted that place to still exist. It was so cool that it was here. It was so great you could get that stuff around here. In Nashville. And so I emailed some places. I tried to reach out to people. Talk to them and see if anyone was interested in hosting that kind of micro-business in town. The Groove was the only place that responded. So we got it up and running. Our shelf, now two, of indie comics and zines.

***Why DO you do this? What keeps ya going?**
Now that I kinda got it, it's not as much work. At first, it was like I had to buy a ton. I had to start up all these relationships from scratch. That's kind of

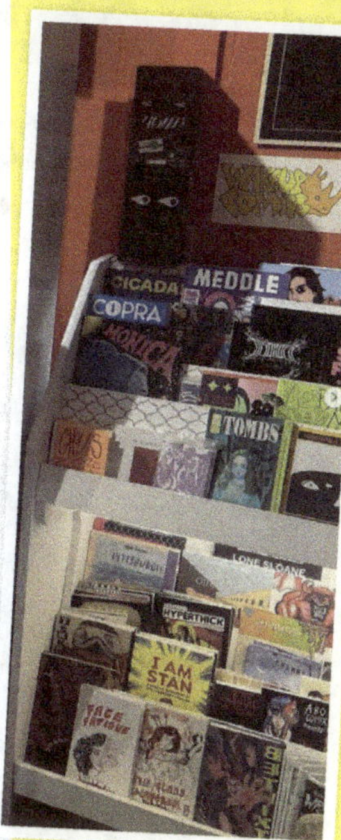

Corporate headquarters
Wake Up Comics Inc.,
Josh Lambert Esq., CEO,
CFO

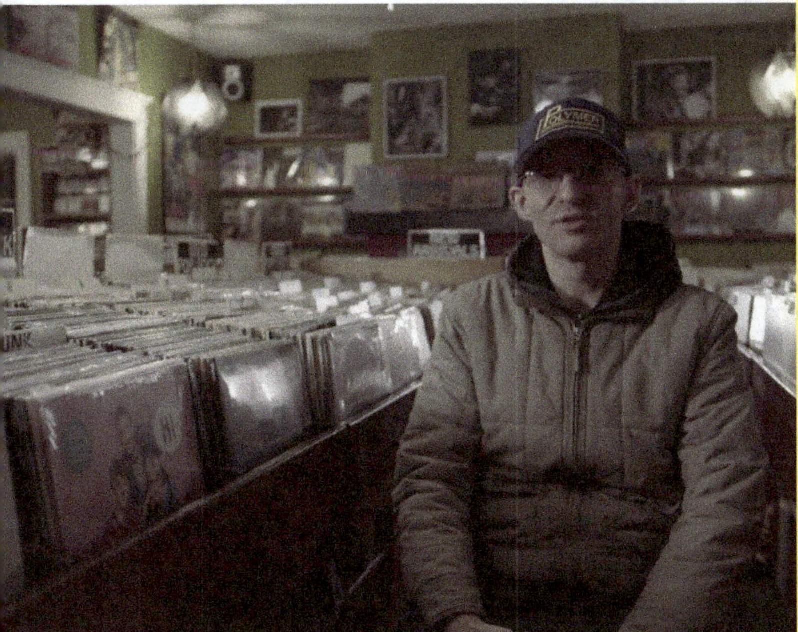

"On The Lam"
Lambert
recording critical
instructions to his
faithful "Wakers" from
*the safoty of **The***
Grove Record Store
bunker / storefront in
Nashville, TN.

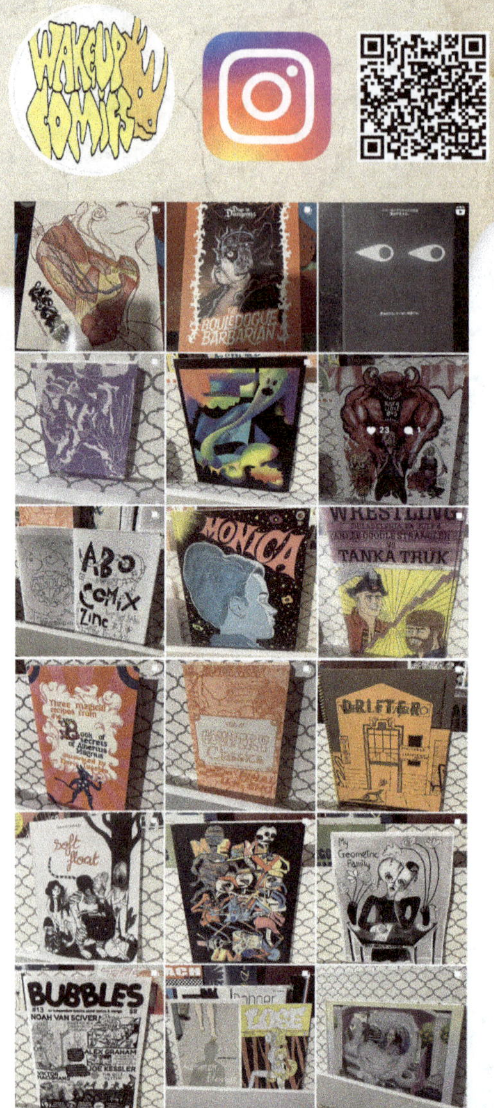

weird but it's also maybe a little bit easier because it's indie comics and artists. You just ask. Just email them about selling their books and they're like sure. All I had to do was say 'Hey, I'm openning this store I'm gonna sell indie stuff. Would you be interested? Maybe sell to me at wholesale?' That's all you gotta do, but I had to go through that whole process. I had to learn all that. Establish those connections. And I had a small budget. I had to be okay with losing money. I said to myself, okay, if I lose all this money… I'm fine. I mean if I never sell them. I knew that it was something that was gonna take my time and my money. I work another full-time job which allows me to do this because I'm not worried about making money so I can buy books that I can break even on and sell that I wouldn't be able to do if I was really worried about my balance sheet. But I just love comics, I guess. What I would say and I really wanted that place to exist here. I felt really lucky to have a place like that once with BrainFreeze. I never would've thought of it. I'm so glad he said that up with that business model. And I'm so glad that The Groove has allowed me to stay there because they could have anything in that spot, and it would probably make them more money. Like literally anything. I think fortunately there's a lot of people that appreciate it. It's a great outlet because those comics are just not out there in the wild. There's really not very many places like WakeUp.

***What is the Future for WakeUp Comics?**
I have thought about this probably too much, but it might just be what it is now. There might not be more to it, you know. I think that would be okay. I'm not a crazy ambitious person and the fact that I was able to get it going, and it's still here six years later is kind of surprising. I do have to put time into it and I can do this thing. I can keep buying books and hopefully not lose money. I don't really make any money from it. It's… I can import books and I can also get books that people can buy so they don't have to pay to import them. They can discover new things. There aren't a lot of people like me and looking at this crap all day long and trying to find new and strange stuff. Reading the comics journal every day. But I do this because there are people out there trying to find new comics. And I love finding new creators I can buy from. Discovering new things. I like that, you know, people told me that they find new stuff here all the time. Stuff they'd never heard of. And I do like that I can provide…or…that I'm kind of providing a service, I don't know. I don't really think of it that way but I am doing what I do. So what's the future like? I might try to move it somewhere else… but I think I would have be forced out of The Groove to do that. I think, you know, maybe, I just keep doing what I'm doing.

*Have you ever thought about getting into PUBLISHING for yourself? Running a Kickstarter?

I will be this year. I have a plan for a like a behind the scenes book but it's going to be higher production. It's going to be a critical appraisal also celebration of the comic COPRA. It's that's gonna be the first thing I try to publish myself. I've commissoned a lot of the articles and art. Most of it is already here. It's been coming in over the past year and so that's gonna be my first project.. But I don't know it's gonna be physically printed. I hope it will be. It will definitely be digital, but since I'm the one paying for it. All for me as far as paying the artist and the writers that just depends on the money. How much will printing be? But that's the first thing I'm gonna do that I thought about doing not necessarily COPRA, but various kind of stages. I was kind of inspired by this project called Critical Chips, which is a few several years old now they were two volumes of it that Zainab Akhtar did. It was really cool. It was kind of like an independent writing thing, but it was more just about comics in general, but I love critical writing about comics. So I got some of the best writers to write about COPRA and it's gonna be really cool. I hope it's gonna be awesome. I've never done anything like this before but I'm gonna do maybe something like a smaller scale after that. Maybe something I do more myself. We'll see how the first one goes.

*ANYTHING YOU HAVEN'T GOTTEN TO SAY THAT THE SMALL NUMBER OF INDIE ARTISTS READING THIS NEED TO HEAR?

Yeah, so… Comics and indie comics is not always the best field financially or anything. But there's so many great comics being published now and just being able to stock and sell some of them to a wider audience is great. I'm glad that all those people are still out there doing them even if it's not a financial thing.. it's more of an artistic thing which is probably for the better. So yeah, just keep on doing what you're doing and hopefully maybe one day indie comics might take over the world, but who knows.

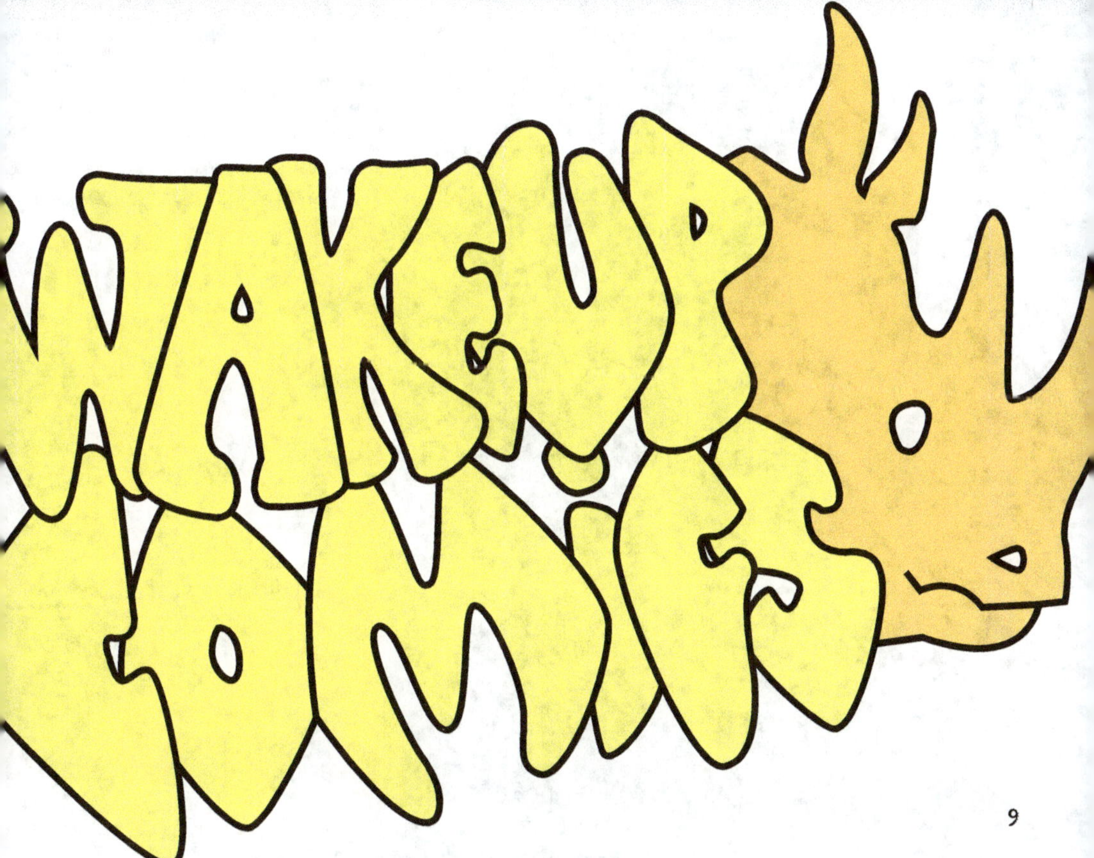

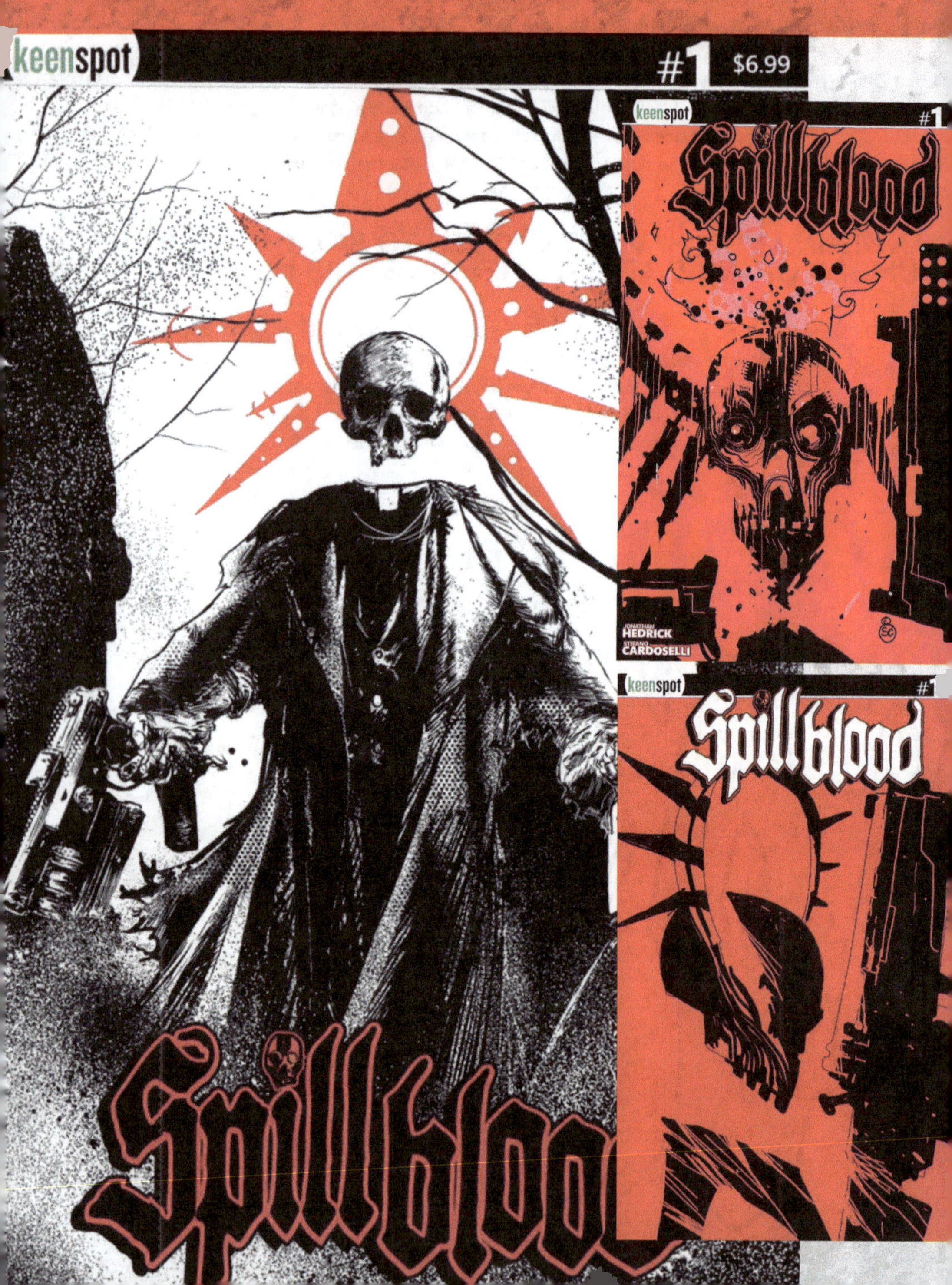
ND OF THE MONTH
with S.K Madden
keenspot
#1 $6.99
keenspot   #1
Spillblood
JONATHAN HEDRICK
STEFANO CARDOSELLI
keenspot   #1
Spillblood
Spillblood

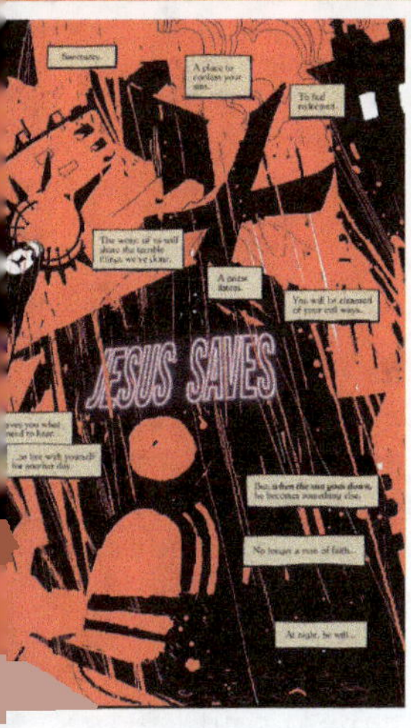

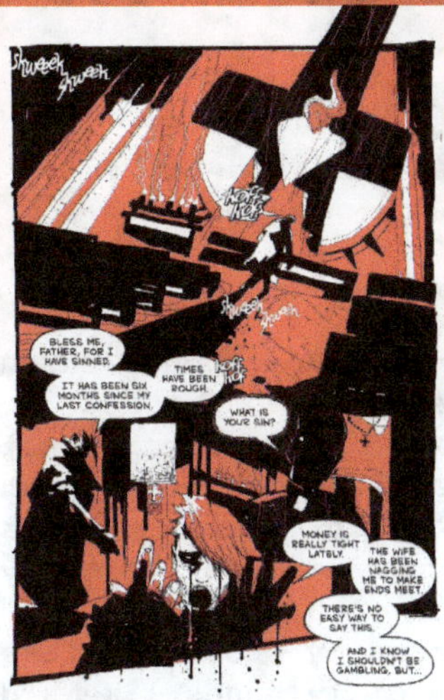

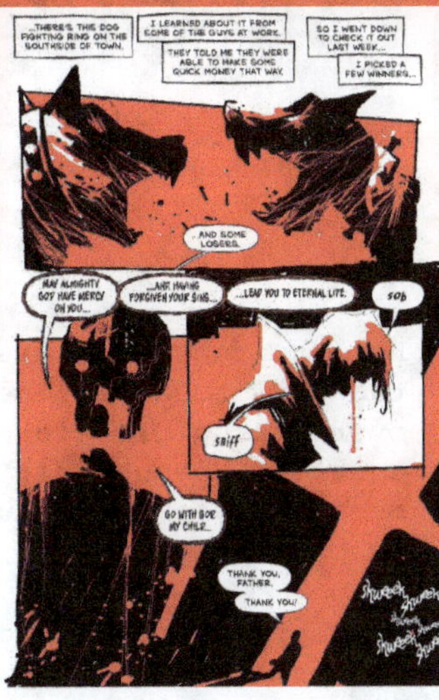

KEENSPOT PRESENTS: SPILLBLOOD

The criminal and the divine clash in a bright and bloody mess in writer Jonathan Hendrick and artist Stefano Cardoselli's horror tale SPILLBLOOD, a 36 page one-shot centered around a community's confessions and the priest-slash-demonic force that hunts down the evildoers who profit off of his wayward flock. The art almost exclusively uses red, black, and white, with a heavy simplification of value and shadow that calls to mind the clean and iconic work of Mike Mignola. The color choices work for the creepy tone of the piece, and the artwork is rendered in an impressionistic way that forgoes a traditional reliance on perspective in favor of emotion and scale. In particular, I enjoy the way the clouds, cityscape, and rain are frequently comixed together, especially in the work's opening scenes when the mystery of Spillblood's mission is still unfolding.

Leo McGovern's lettering is a standout storytelling tool in the one-shot. It frequently carries the narrative tension through a scene, stamping bold and cutting special effects at just the right place in the panel. As the story unfolds and Spillblood continues on its murderous rampage, McGovern deftly employs a variety of lettering techniques to execute the deep, powerful growl of fighting dogs, incessant storms of gunshots, and the hiss of newly lit molotov cocktail. The muted golden-brown background that backs the narration also helps balance out the sometimes monotonous hues and values in the comic.

While the stark and vibrant crimson gives the comic a horrific punch, the effect of this choice weakened for me as the story went on and I became increasingly desensitized to the vibrancy of the limited palette. There is a pink color Cardoselli uses in the opening third of the comic that trickles out of the story, and once it's gone entirely I found myself sorely missing it. The things about the linework I did enjoy – the tears falling down a confessor's face, the zipper of a man's tracksuit, the loose and circular depiction of clouds and smoke – tend to get buried in the loose and jarring style.

Unfortunately, I found this to be doubly true for Hendrick's writing, which loses tension as the story unfolds due to its rather routine nature. SPILLBOOD is essentially three separate stories. In each one, Spillblood listens to someone confess a crime, then appears at the scene of the crime, and executes the criminals – usually in a rain of gunfire. There's no real mystery or puzzle Spillblood must solve, it simply shows up and enacts violence. There's also no overarching narrative tension to buoy the scenes, so once I finished the second story I already knew the remaining ten pages would play out the exact same way as the previous twenty. Because of this I lost interest in the finale before it had even begun, when I should be the most engaged. Artistically stylish but rather repetitive, SPILLBLOOD never quite elevates to a satisfying conclusion.

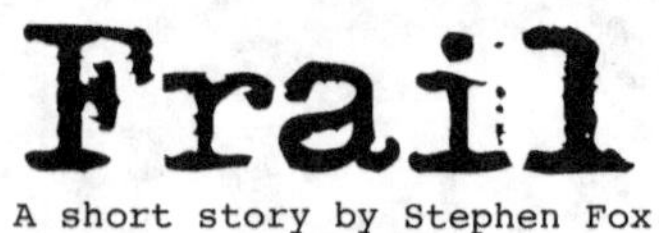

Frail

A short story by Stephen Fox

Chapter 1: Kin

How the fuck did this happen? Rain pours through the bare trees that fill the space between my dead parents' home, and the bluff overlooking Old Hickory Lake. Giant drops spatter against my head and roll through dirty hair and forehead sweat; the mixture sets my eyes burning. Diluted blood covers my hands. The leaves under my boots may as well be covered in oil — everything's sliding.

I wrap my fingers hard around my brother's forearm. The pressure causes his arm to flip out of my hands like a desperate trout. His whole body slides back down onto a sharp shoot of wood now cutting through his right oblique. He shrieks in agony as the rough bark snags and grabs his organs, flesh, and skin. I tumble back. A few saplings crack in two as I fall. I'd pushed my leather satchel to my back — it takes the brunt. Gravity drags me toward the edge. Old Hickory Lake is about fifty feet away — straight down past this last line of trees.

Despite Neil being pinned down by the tree, he still scares the shit out of me. It's been a hell of a night — there's no knowing what he might do if I wander within reach. He glares at me. I wrap my hands backward around a couple of nearby branches, and gently pull my weight forward — back to the last stretch of level ground.

"I'm gonna fucking strangle you." Neil growls. His breathing is wet. Blood runs down a fat line of dark red from his chin. Panic blanks his words. My hands are numb. Heartbeats shake through me. I can't slow my breathing — drowning in adrenaline.
I close my eyes and push hard against a sturdy tree trunk behind me while pulling against two uncertain branches. "Be quiet, or I'll leave you," I choke out between gasps and grunts. Hate fills his eyes. He raises his hands in mock surrender. After a few jerks forward, I finally gain footing. Okay — what now? The garage. Dad kept all kinds of handy shit there.

Even amidst the chaos, my dad's peg board swells a lump in my throat. The tools hang exactly as they always have — obedient, waiting. Even the "Please put tools back where they belong — Keith Leonard" note is undisturbed and yellowing under several strips of old scotch tape.

Rope. Saw. The wood stabbing through him is only about two inches wide, but that's thick enough. I navigate the unlit path and hang my pack on a short branch a few yards from Neil. I shove my right hand deep in the satchel. It feels like I'm trying to find anything in my mom's purse. Finally, the tip of my index finger finds a steel link on the handcuffs. I drag them out. They pull something else out along the way. I worry a bit as whatever thuds against mud and vanishes under the blanket of dead leaves.

"What the hell are you doing?" Neil's expression shifts to panic
as he catches a glimpse of the restraints. The first cuff is easy,
but I click it a couple of notches too tight. The injury is taking
its toll on him; Neil's slowing down. He tosses a limp swipe at the
other bracelet before his head meets the ground with a soggy thud.
The second cuff ratchets shut. A square knot on the chain between
his wrists should hold.

The banister of the deck will help me pulley him up enough to
saw through the ground-end of the tree. I remember the first aid
training Carrie gave me when the girls were young; leave the branch
in the wound. With a hoist, his back is far enough off the dirt
for me to cut through the small tree. I start cutting; dammit — I
grabbed the wrong saw. No time — saw faster.

Dad built a lot this house. It would've lasted a lifetime — or
should have — if the dipshit on the other end of this rope had
resealed the deck. Twenty feet of spindles and railing pop, crack
and rip toward us. Plans are bullshit.

The banister slams into my chest, pinning me to a nearby tree and
jerking the rope from my hands. Gray, bowed wood zips downward and
drags across my chest — tearing my flannel shirt and ripping into my
skin. I'm rolled between the sliding lumber and the year old maple
behind me. The wood twists around the tree, and an inch to the left
of Neil's unconscious body.

Debris tumbles past me, dragging Neil toward the bluff. The tree in
my brother's gut resists, tearing against his flesh. His head jerks
up. He howls like I've never heard. I scramble to reclaim ground
between us — digging into my wet jean pockets to find the handcuff
keys. I throw myself the last several feet, and try to insert the
key into one of the cuffs. The rope twists Neil's body nearly ninety
degrees; the key pops out of my hands and next to Neil's head. I
grab for it.

Neil bites the hell out of my bare forearm: his teeth dig into
me as the tree tugs against him. I can feel his canines dig into
muscle. My other hand lands on a slick sandstone rock the size of
my hand. I slam it into his forehead. Blood rolls into his eyes and
bubbles under a steaming exhale.

I slam the stone harder. I can't get him to let go. He won't. Then
harder — so hard the impact of the stone shoves his teeth deeper
into me. Again. Again. Again.

(continued in ND Riot #2)

Not Your Pappy's COMICS SECTION

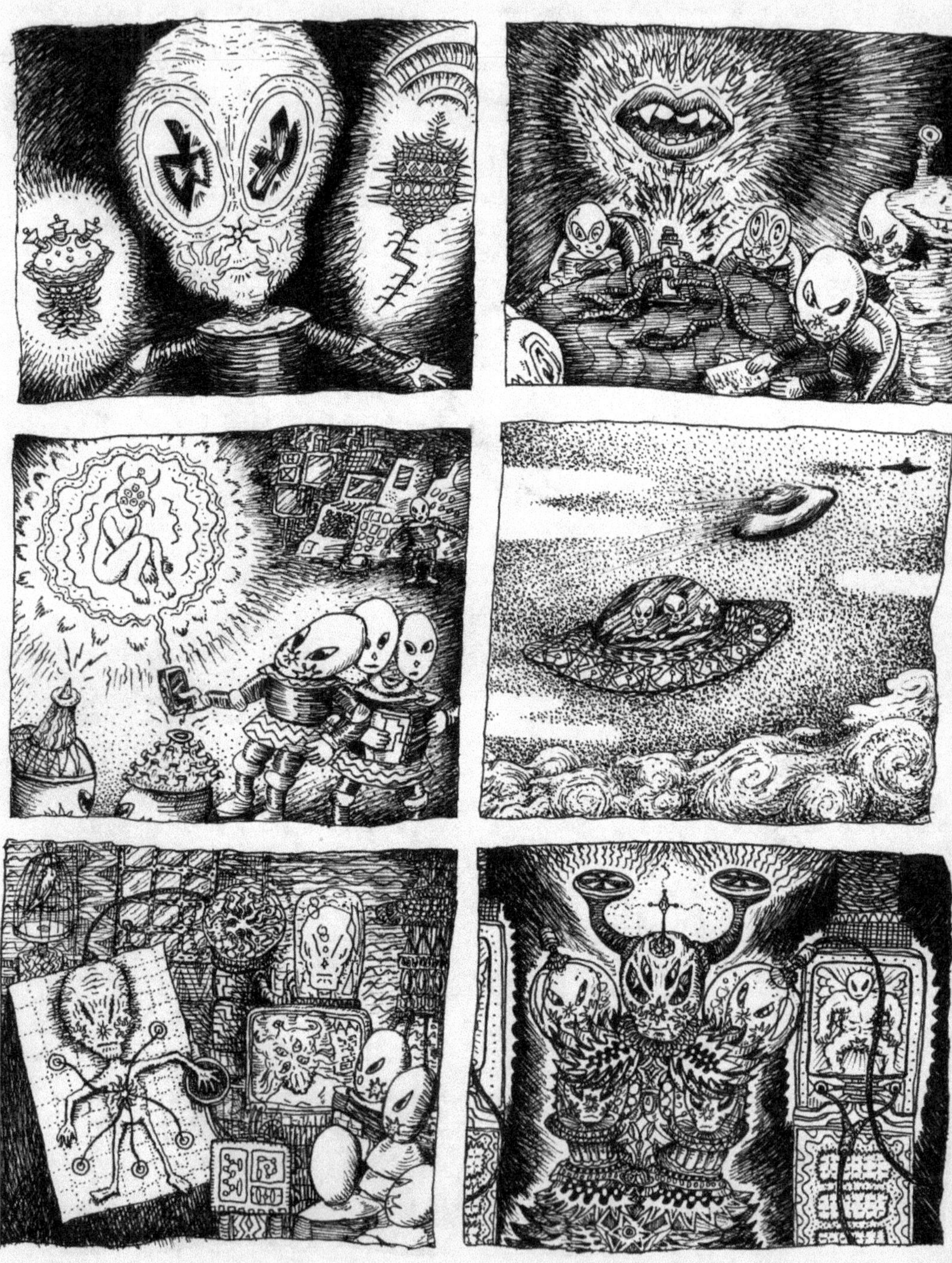

by Benji Anderson

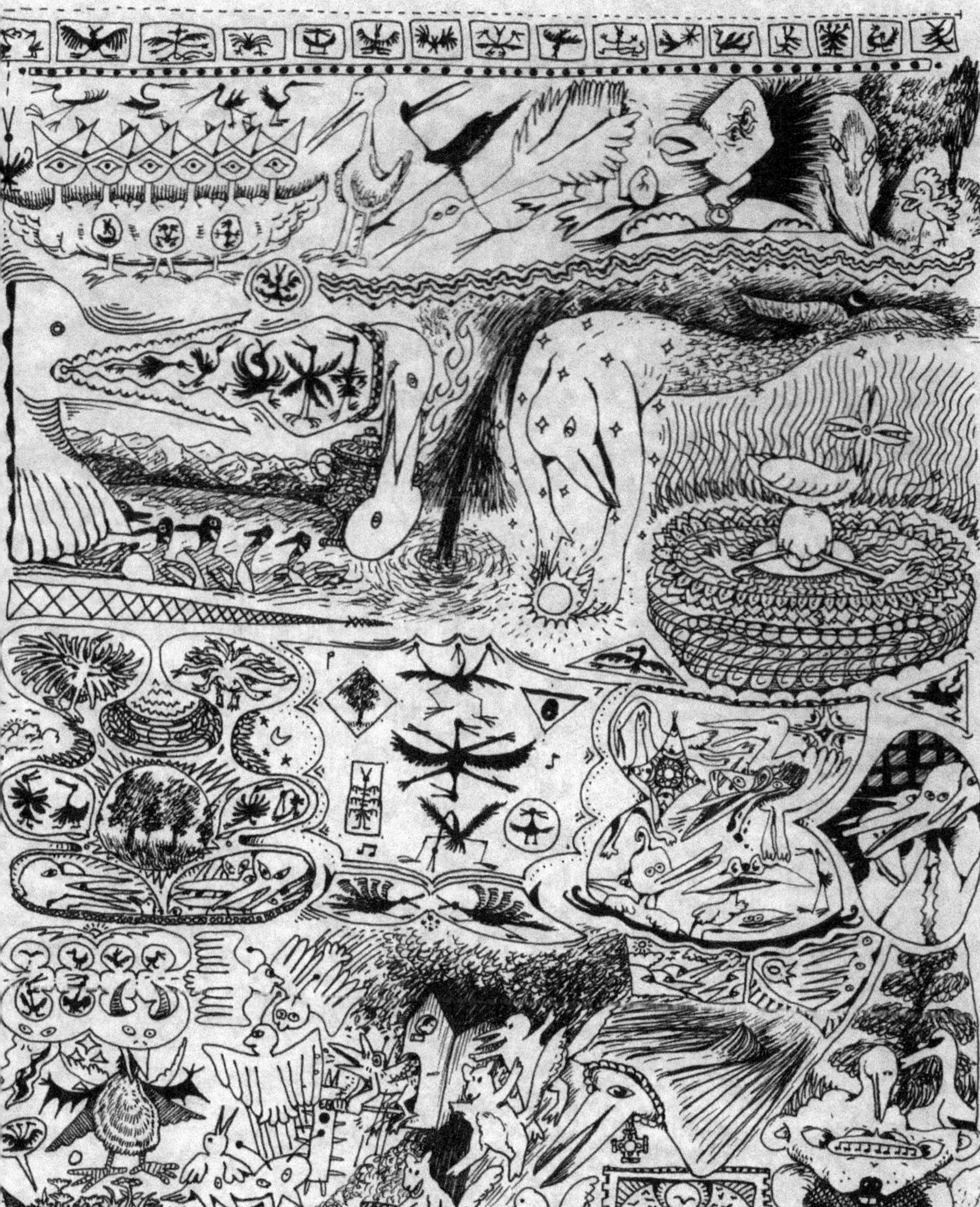

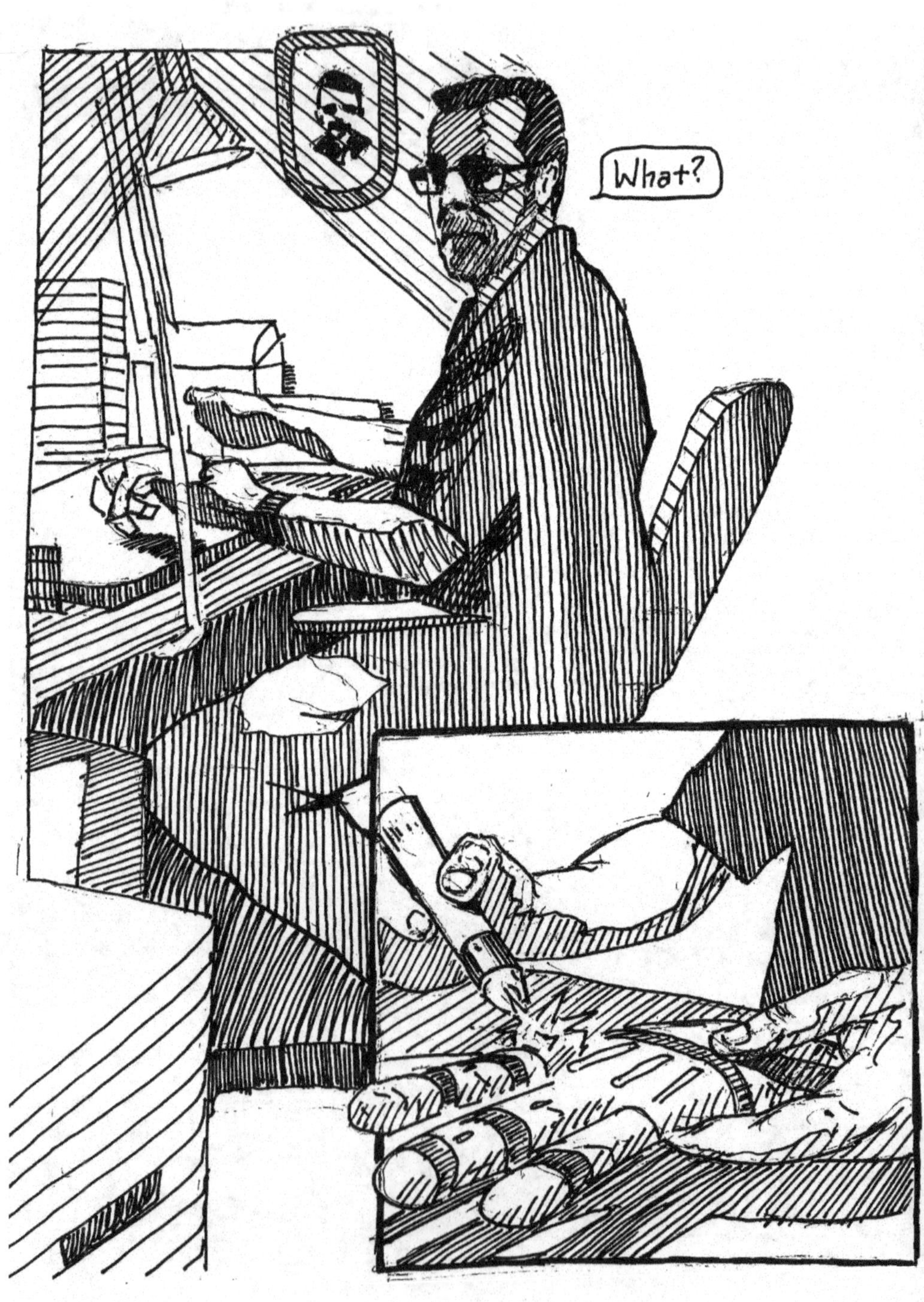
What?

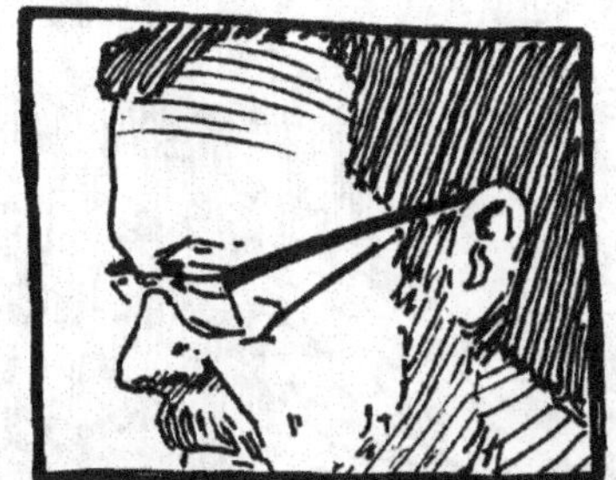

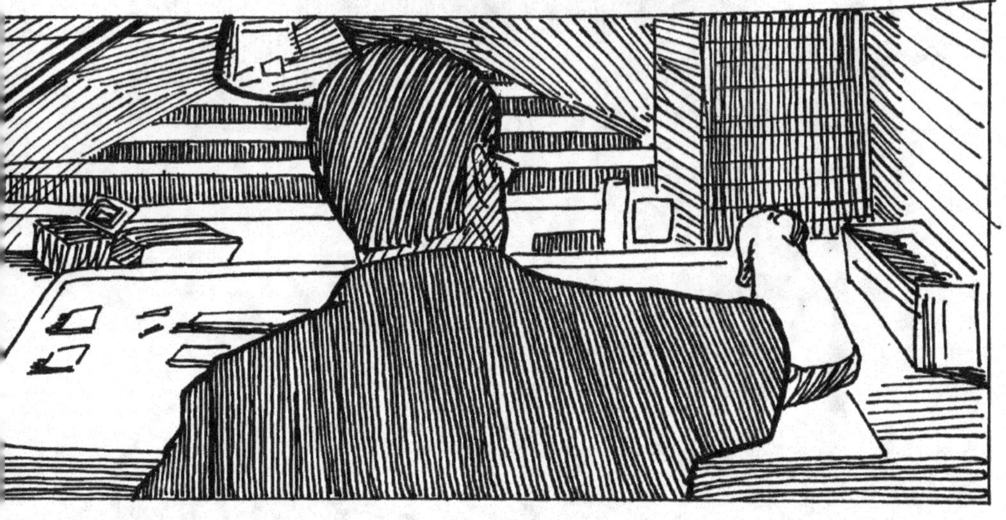

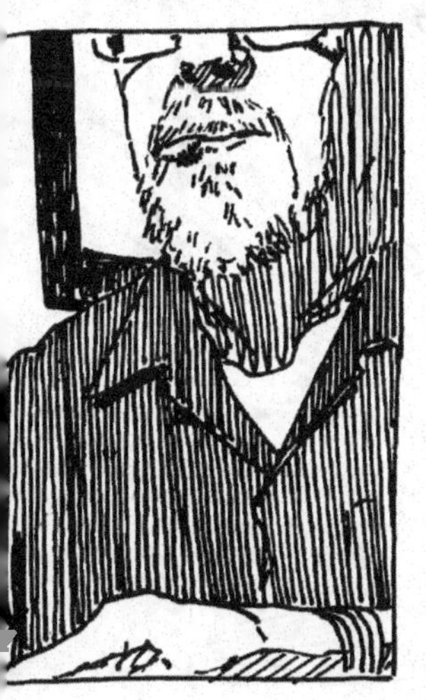

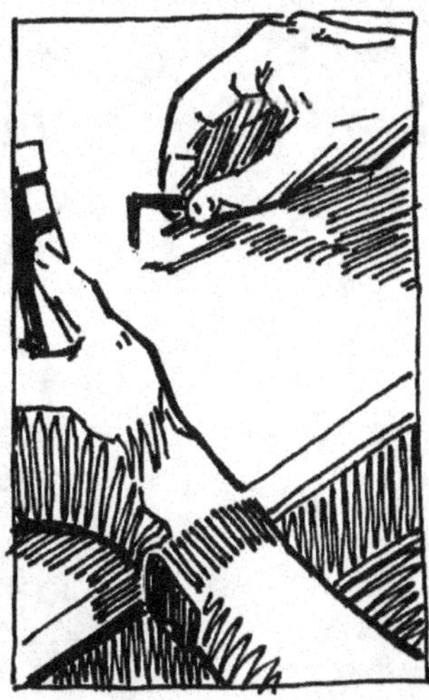

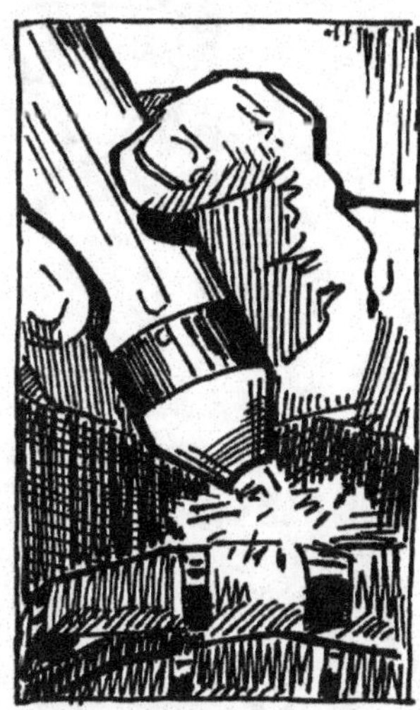

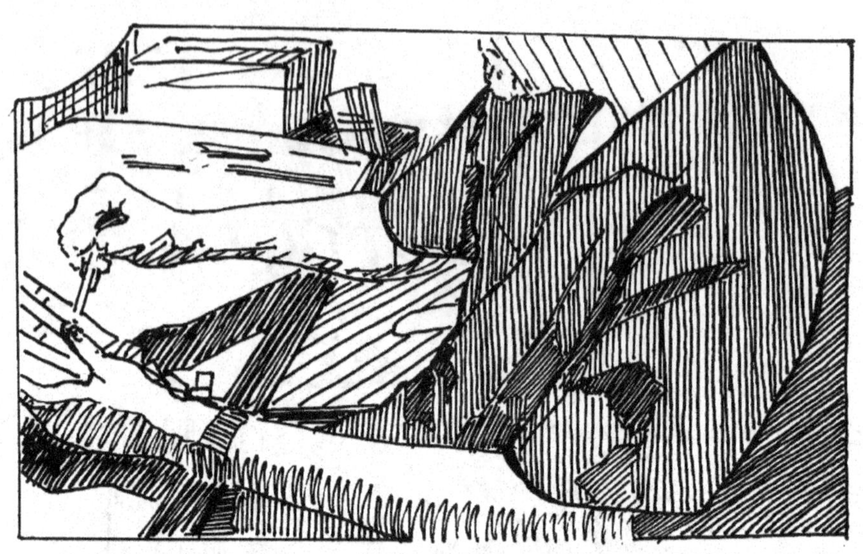

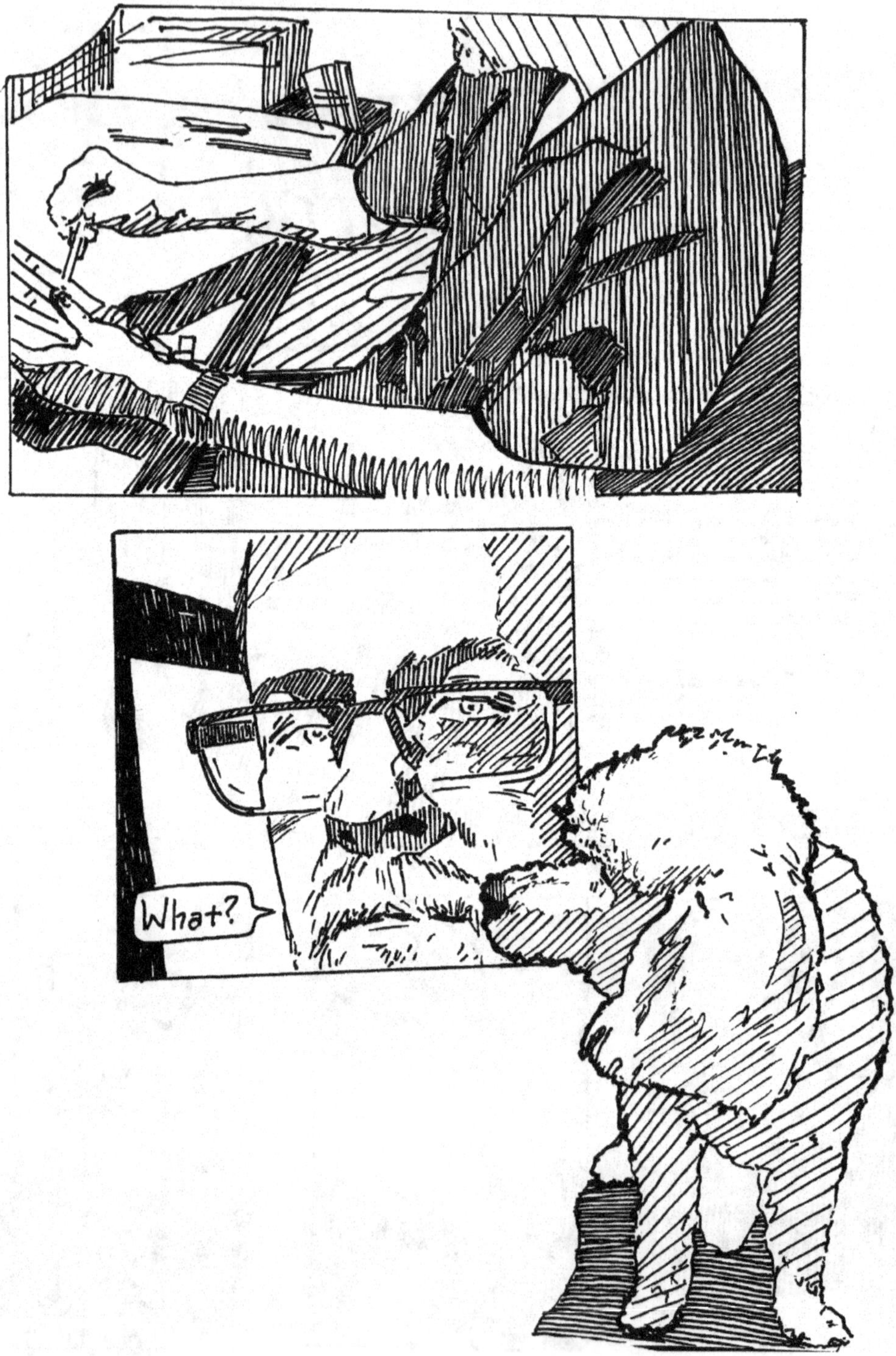

What?

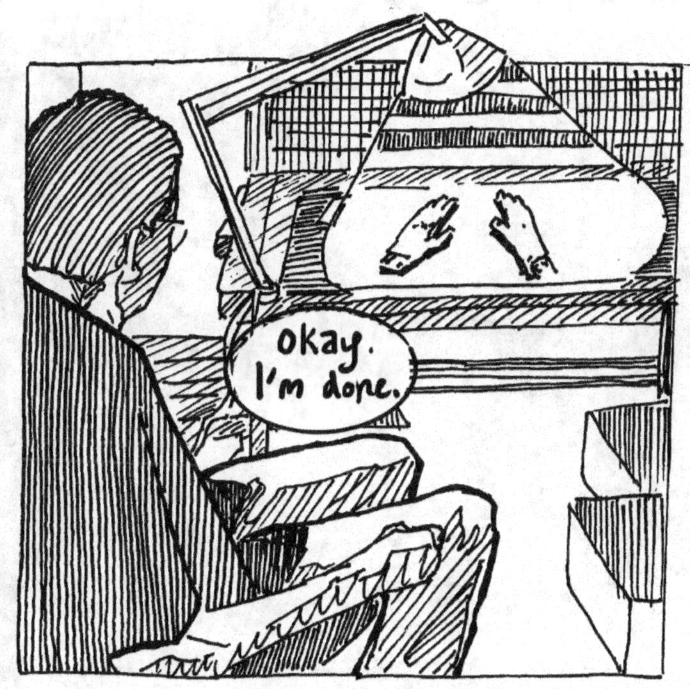
okay.
I'm done.

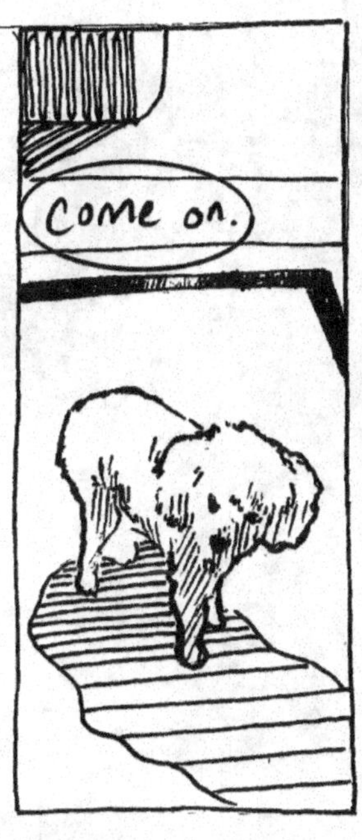
come on.

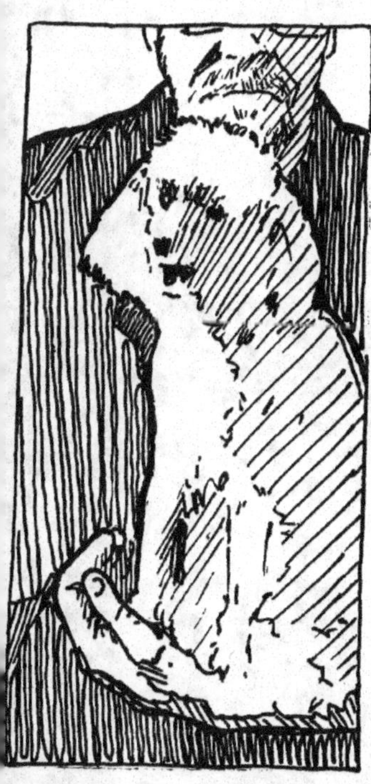

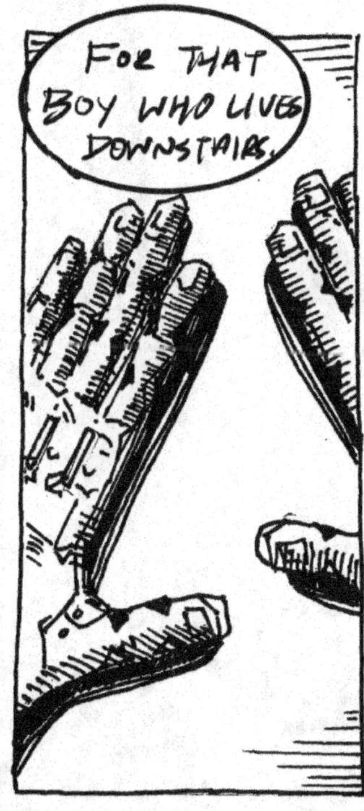
FOR THAT
BOY WHO LIVES
DOWNSTAIRS.

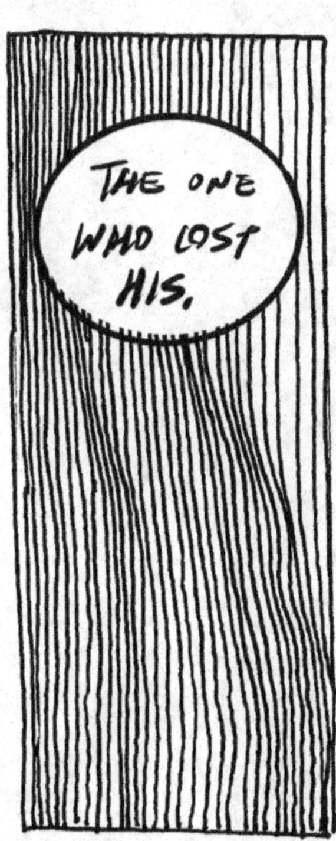
THE ONE
WHO LOST
HIS,

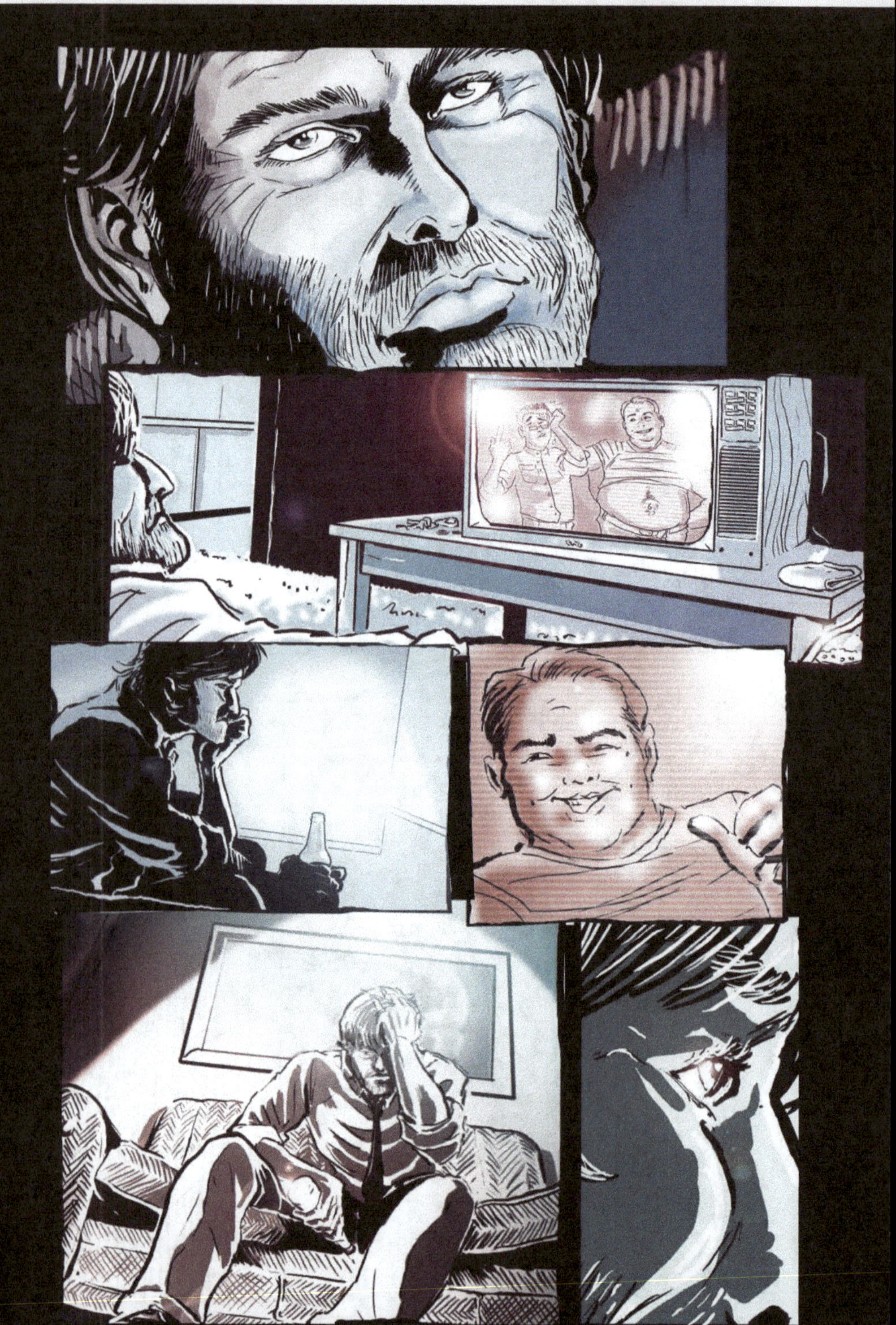

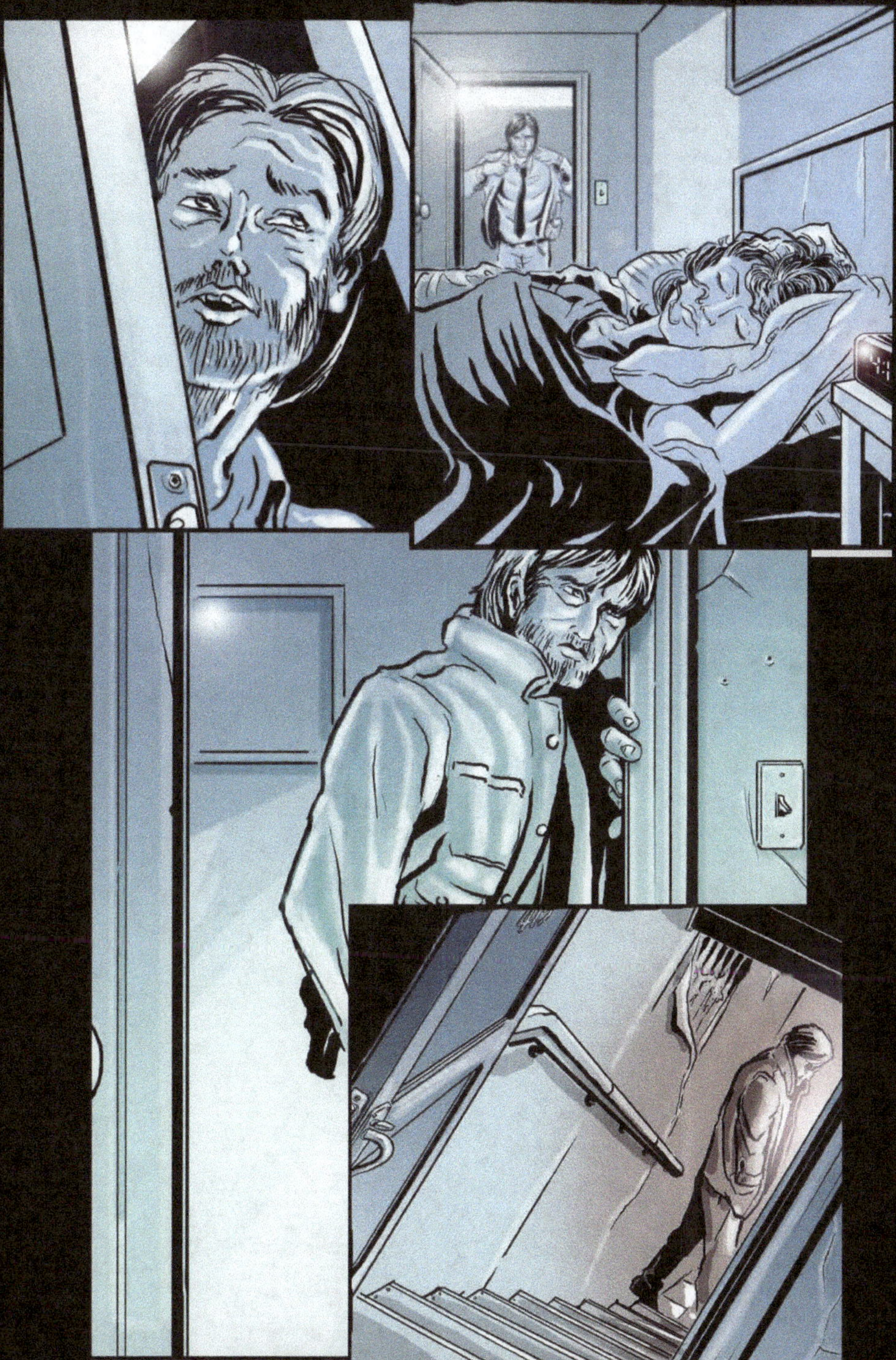

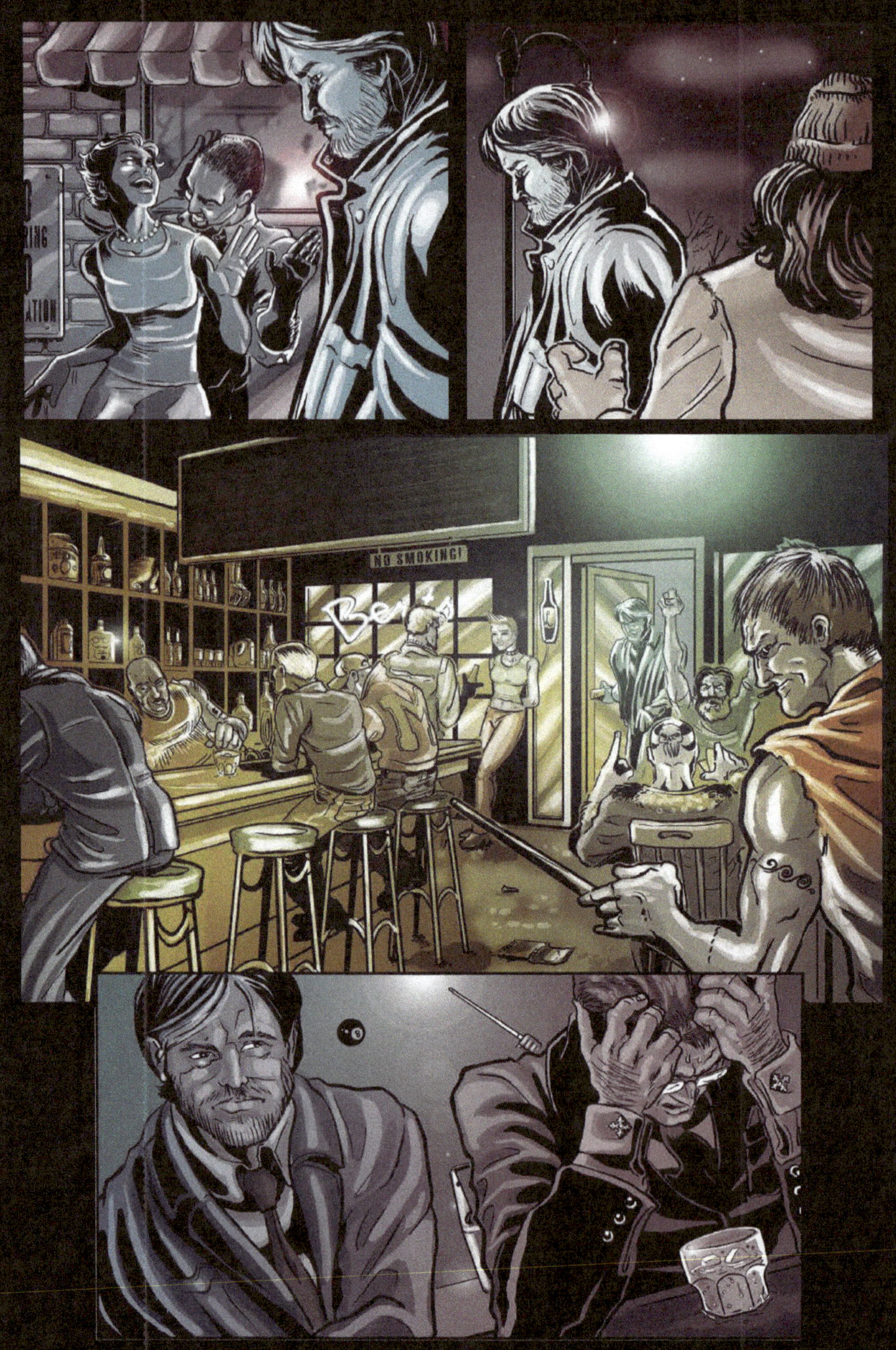

NO SMOKING!

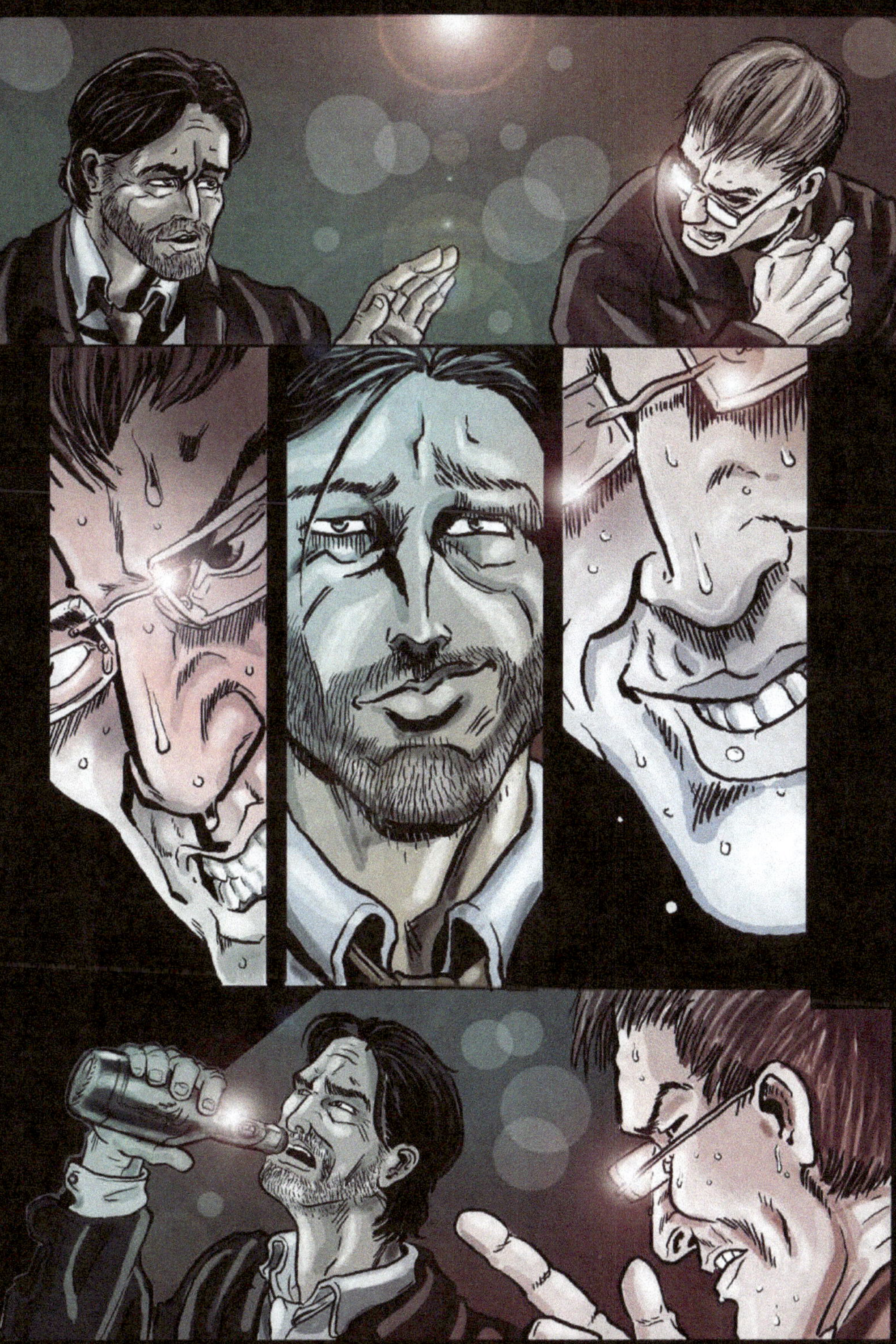

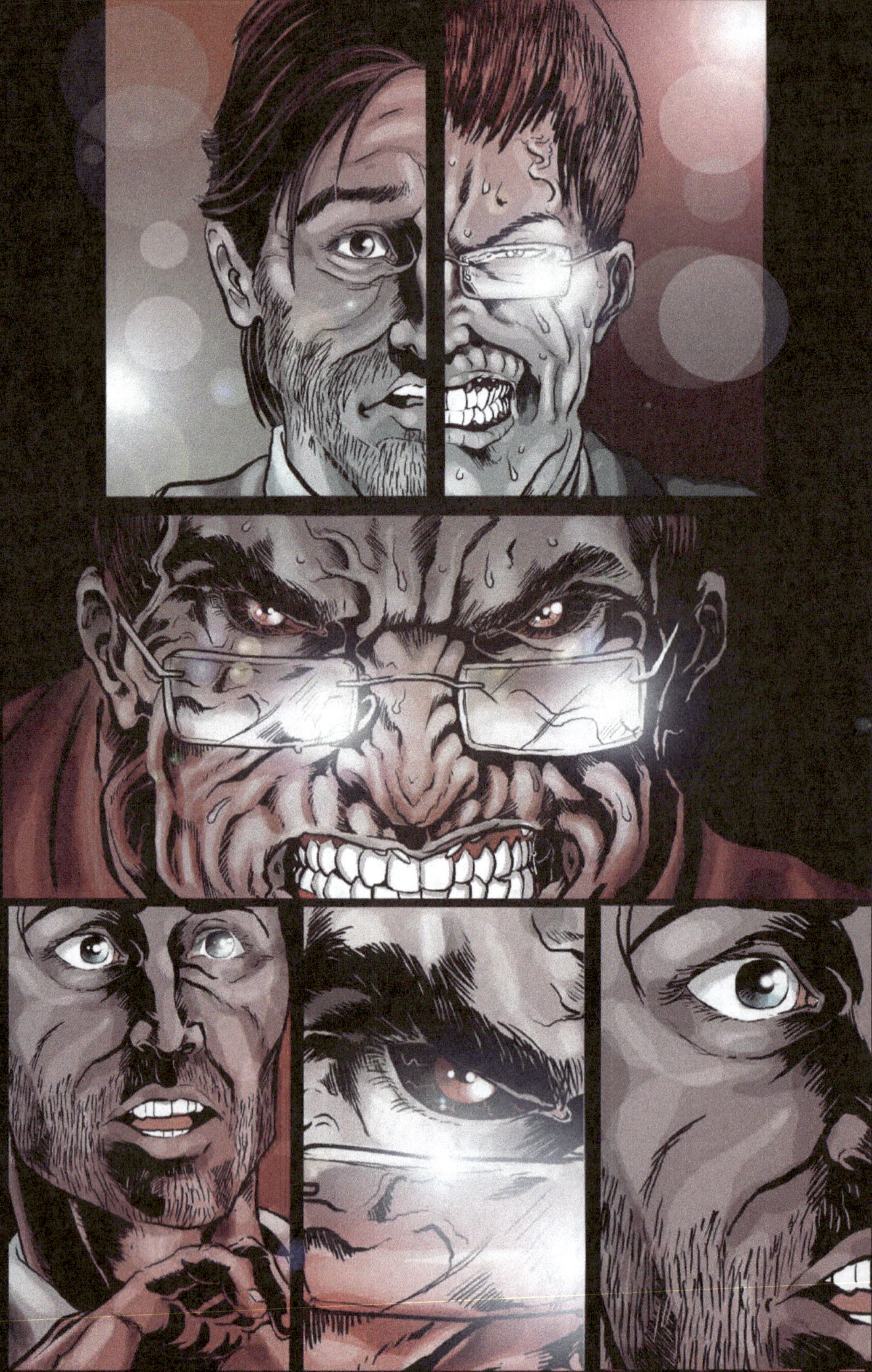

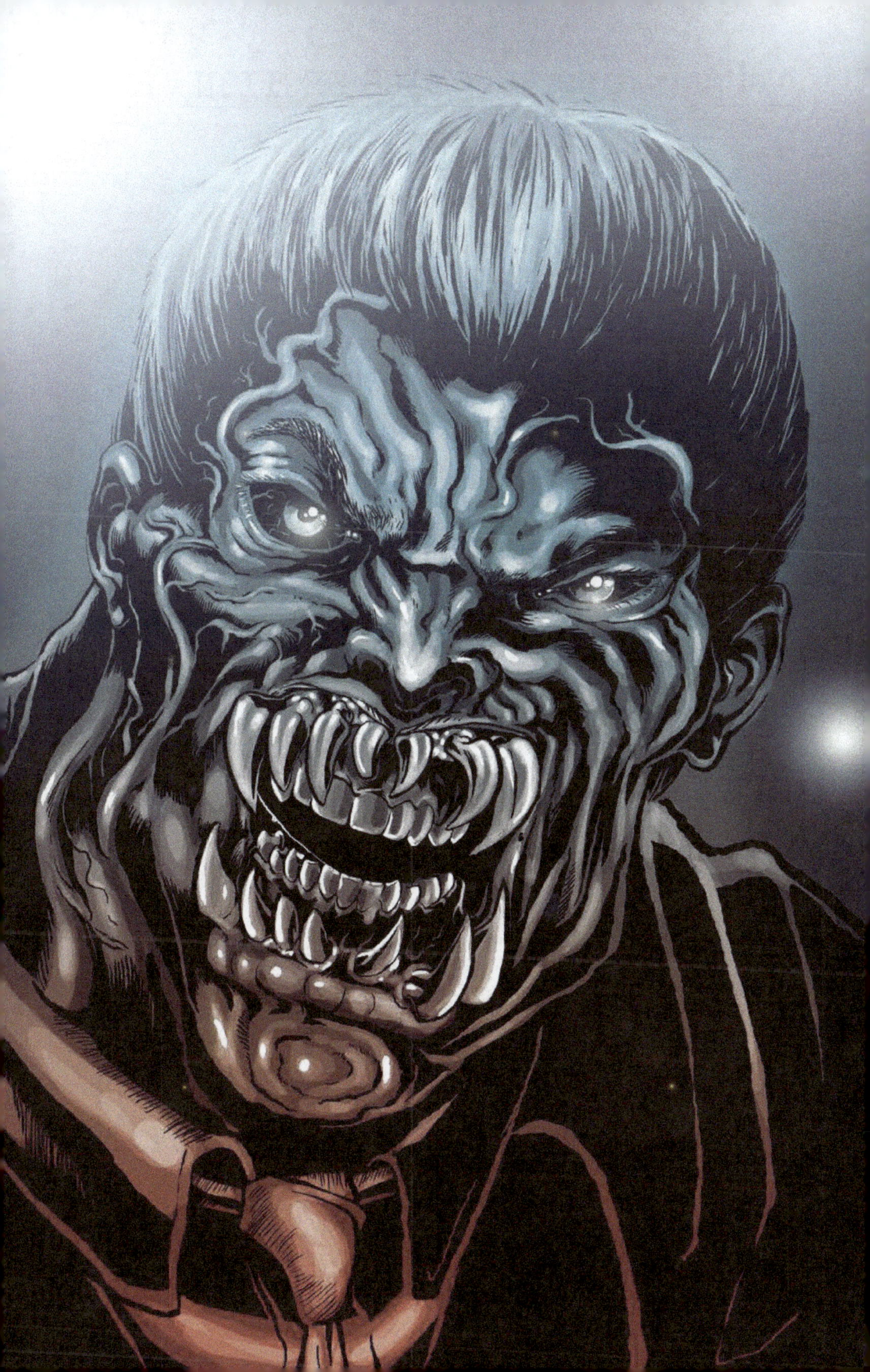

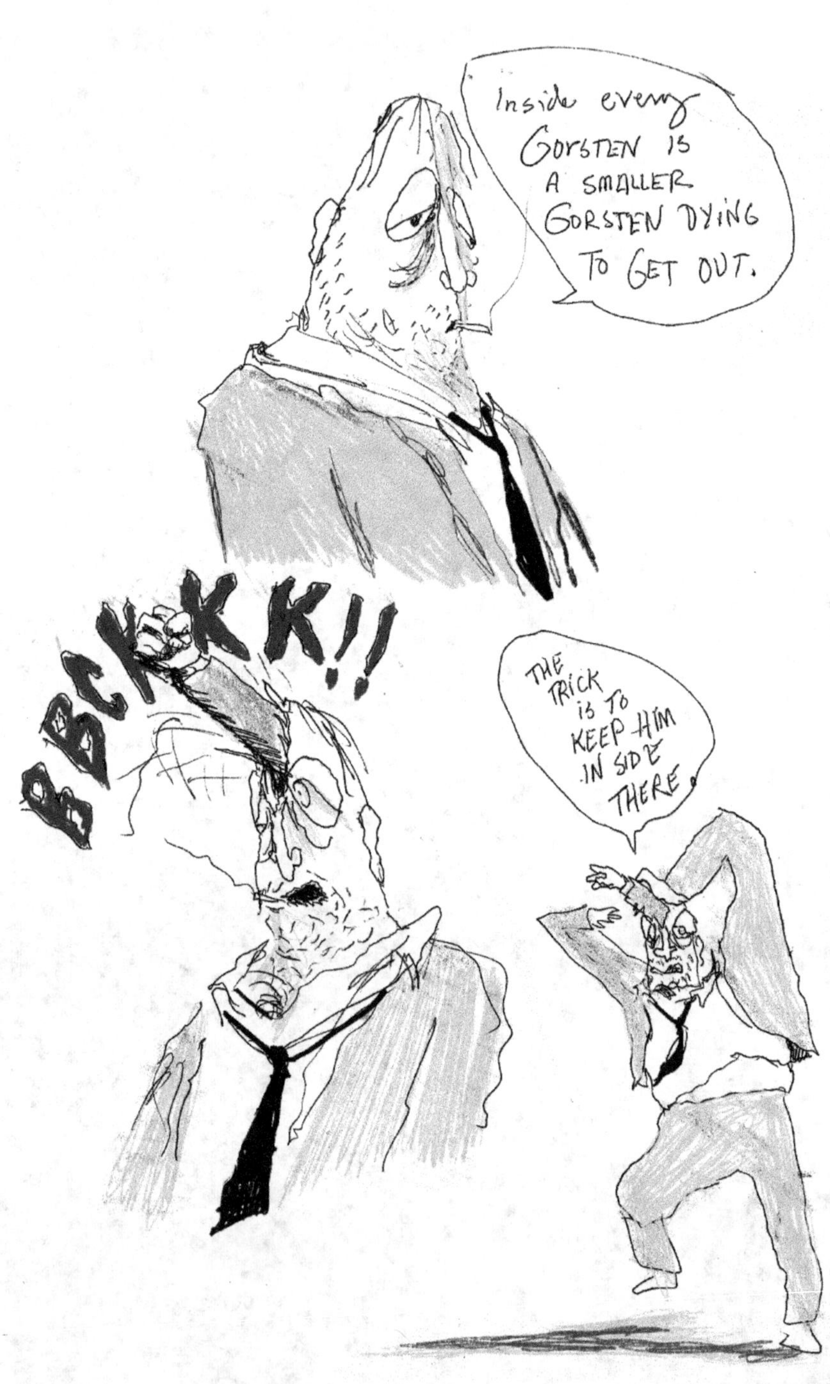
Inside every GORSTEN IS A SMALLER GORSTEN DYING TO GET OUT.
BBCKKK!!
THE TRICK IS TO KEEP HIM INSIDE THERE.

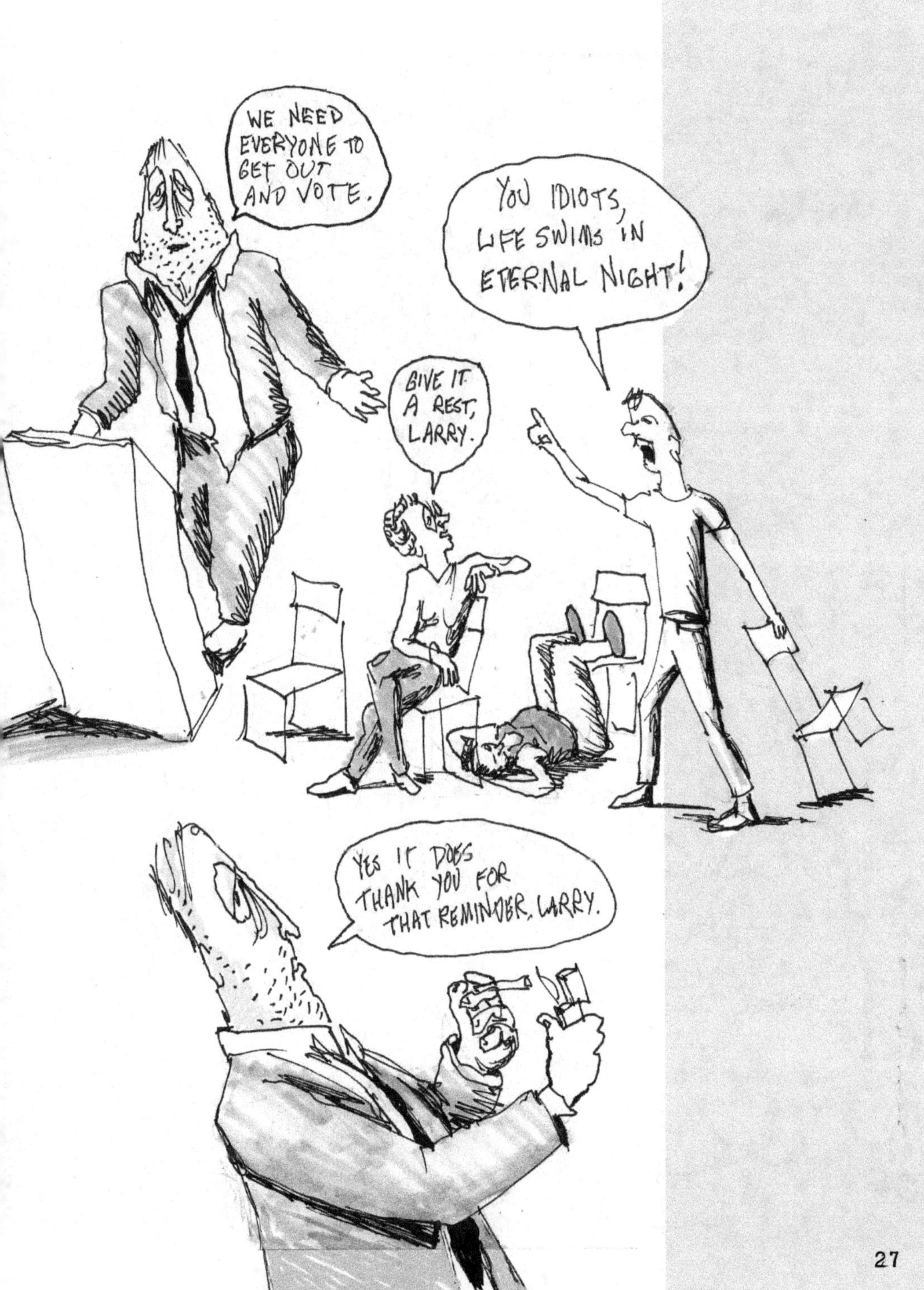
WE NEED EVERYONE TO GET OUT AND VOTE.
YOU IDIOTS, LIFE SWIMS IN ETERNAL NIGHT!
GIVE IT A REST, LARRY.
YES IT DOES THANK YOU FOR THAT REMINDER, LARRY.

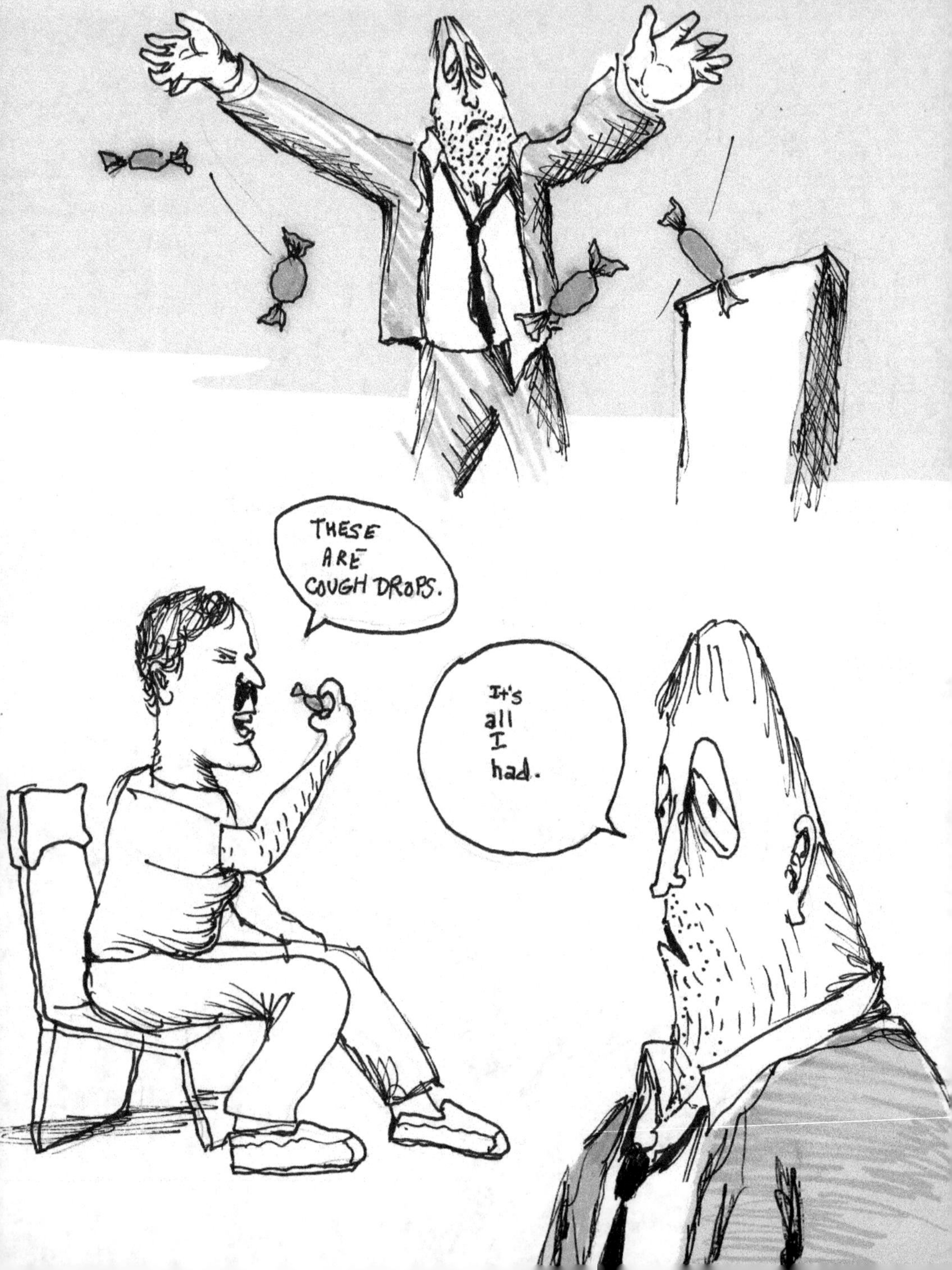

CURE YOUR BLUES WITH CANDEEEE!
THESE ARE COUGH DROPS.
It's all I had.

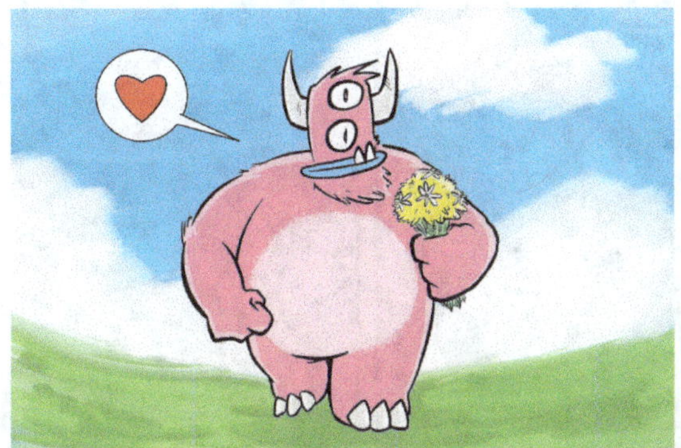

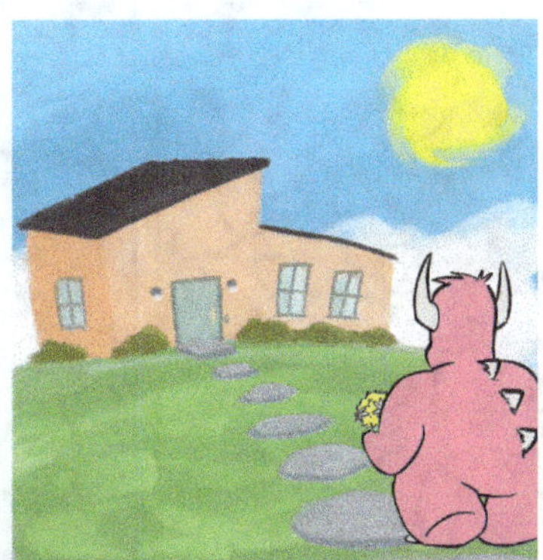

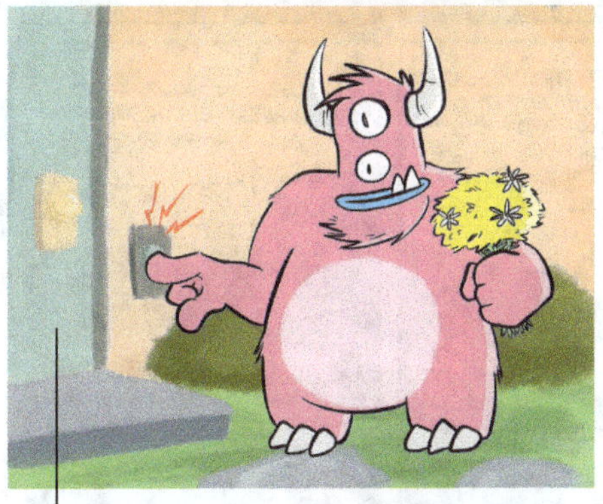

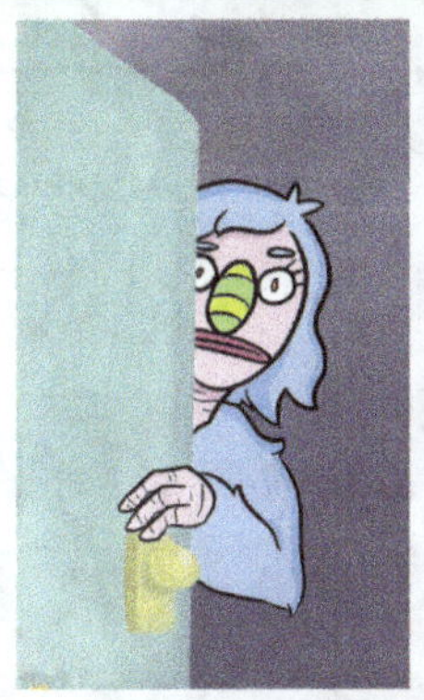

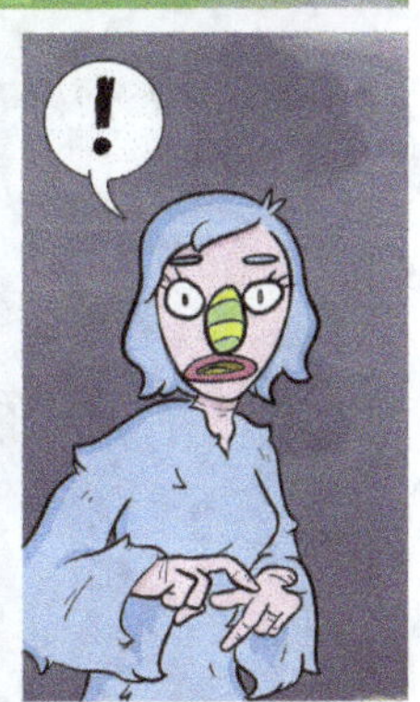

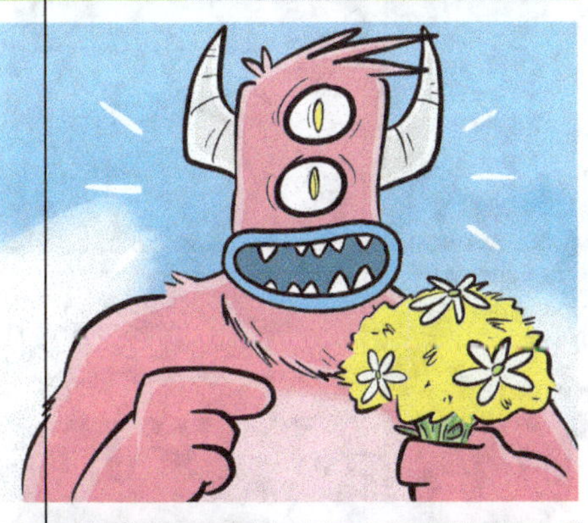

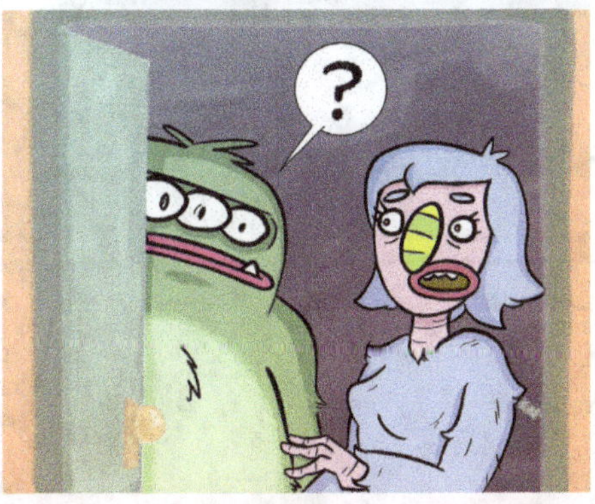

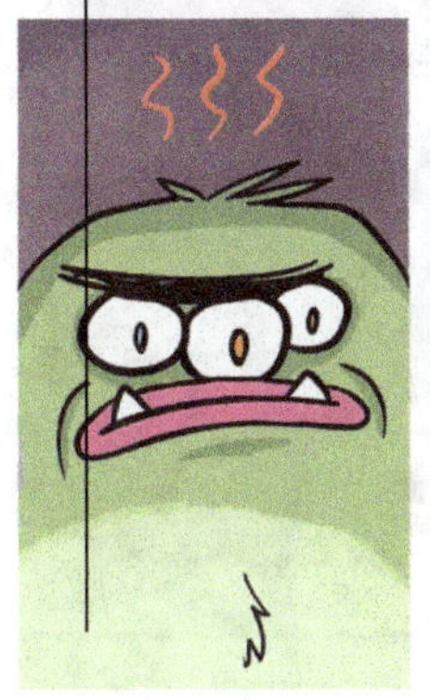

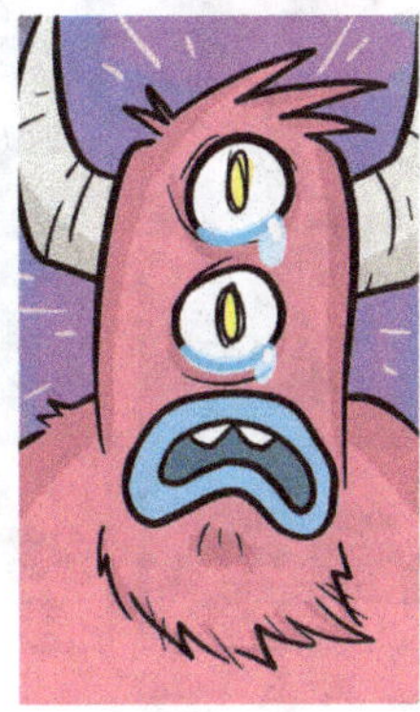

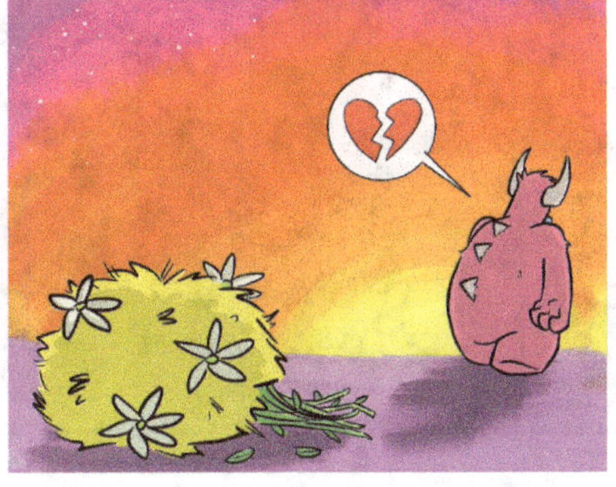

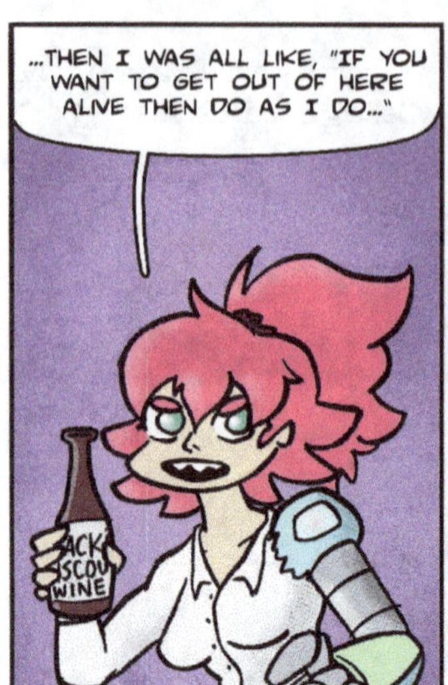
...THEN I WAS ALL LIKE, "IF YOU WANT TO GET OUT OF HERE ALIVE THEN DO AS I DO..."

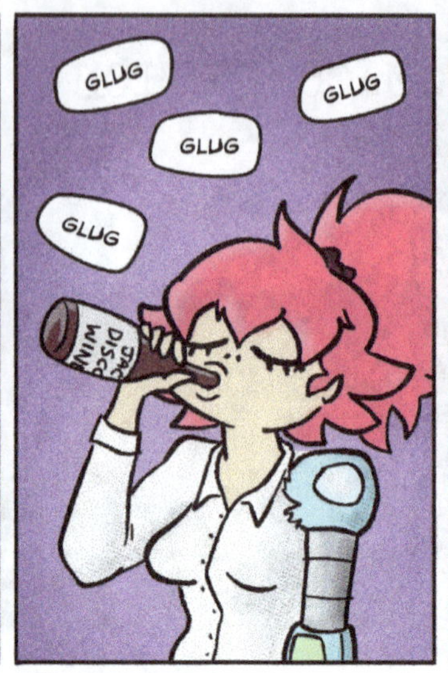
GLUG
GLUG
GLUG
GLUG

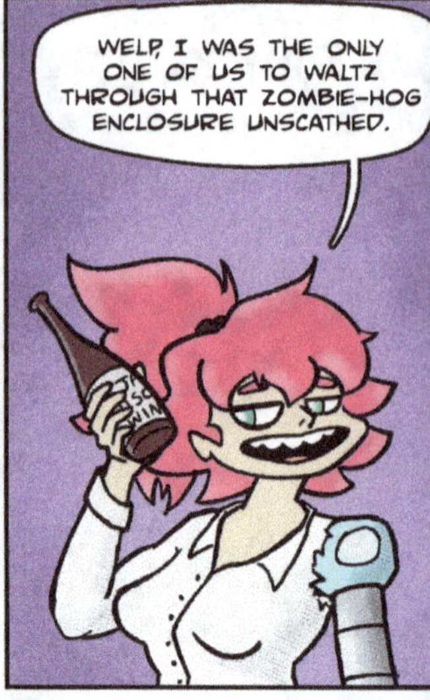
WELP, I WAS THE ONLY ONE OF US TO WALTZ THROUGH THAT ZOMBIE-HOG ENCLOSURE UNSCATHED.

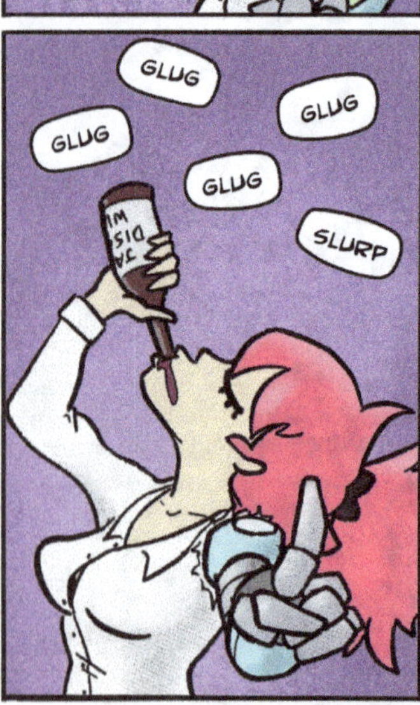
GLUG
GLUG
GLUG
GLUG
SLURP

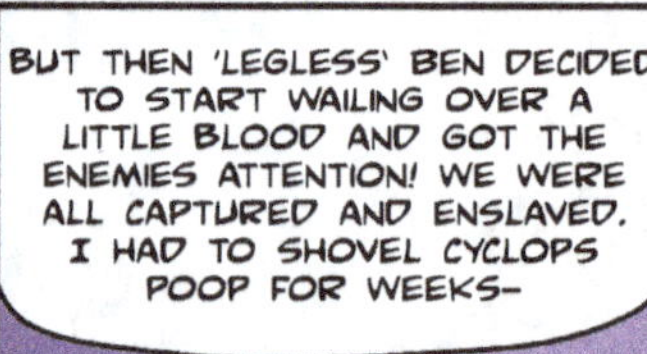
BUT THEN 'LEGLESS' BEN DECIDED TO START WAILING OVER A LITTLE BLOOD AND GOT THE ENEMIES ATTENTION! WE WERE ALL CAPTURED AND ENSLAVED. I HAD TO SHOVEL CYCLOPS POOP FOR WEEKS—

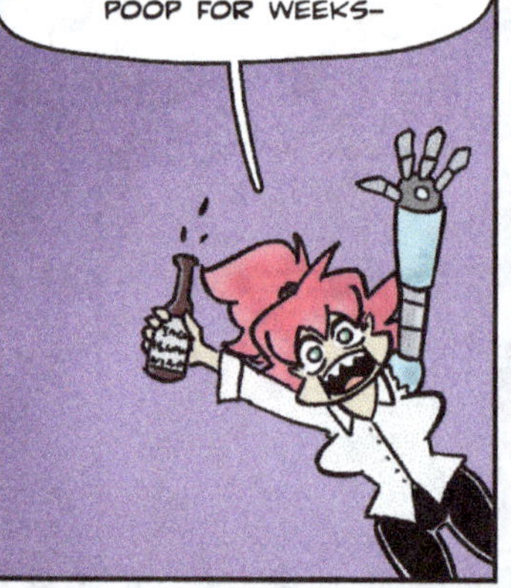

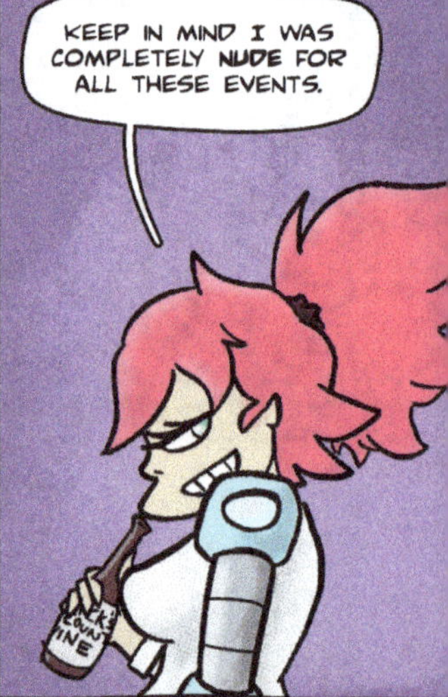
KEEP IN MIND I WAS COMPLETELY NUDE FOR ALL THESE EVENTS.

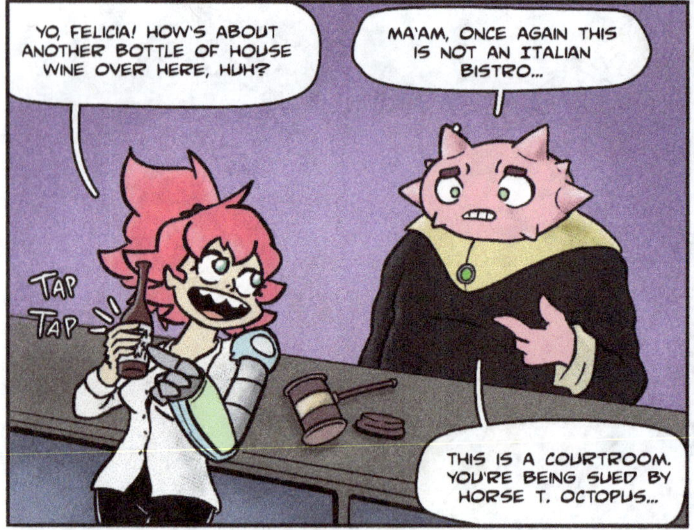
YO, FELICIA! HOW'S ABOUT ANOTHER BOTTLE OF HOUSE WINE OVER HERE, HUH?
MA'AM, ONCE AGAIN THIS IS NOT AN ITALIAN BISTRO...
TAP TAP
THIS IS A COURTROOM. YOU'RE BEING SUED BY HORSE T. OCTOPUS...

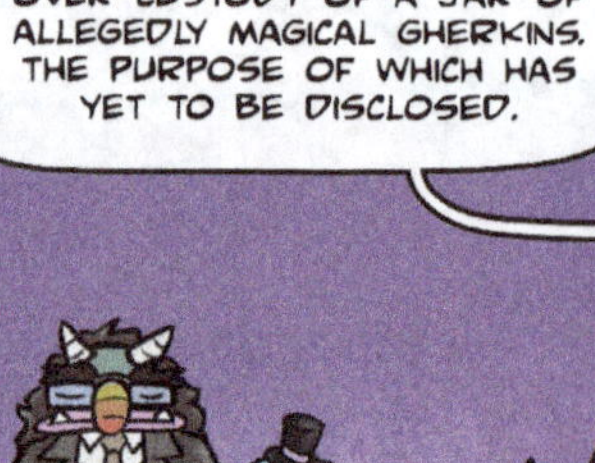
OVER CUSTODY OF A JAR OF ALLEGEDLY MAGICAL GHERKINS. THE PURPOSE OF WHICH HAS YET TO BE DISCLOSED.

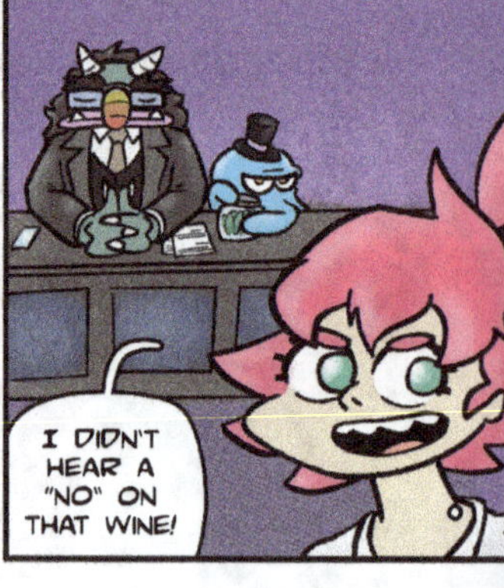
I DIDN'T HEAR A "NO" ON THAT WINE!

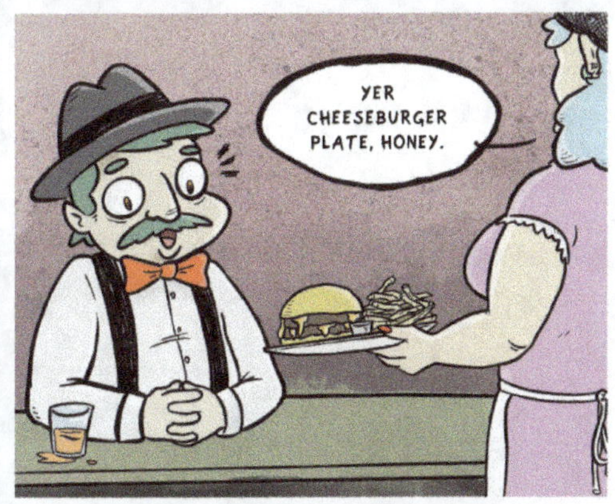

YER CHEESEBURGER PLATE, HONEY.

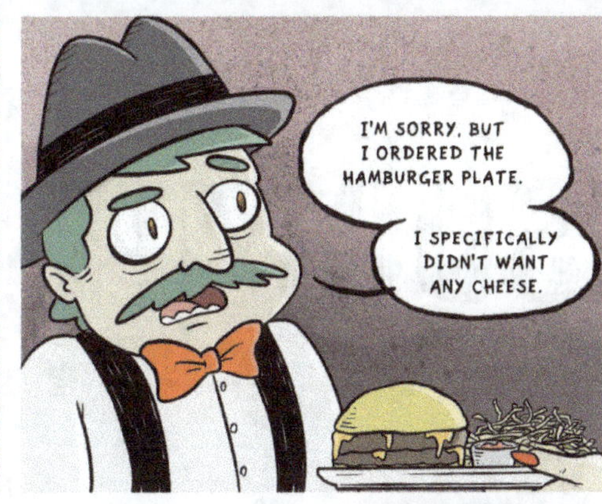

I'M SORRY, BUT I ORDERED THE HAMBURGER PLATE.
I SPECIFICALLY DIDN'T WANT ANY CHEESE.

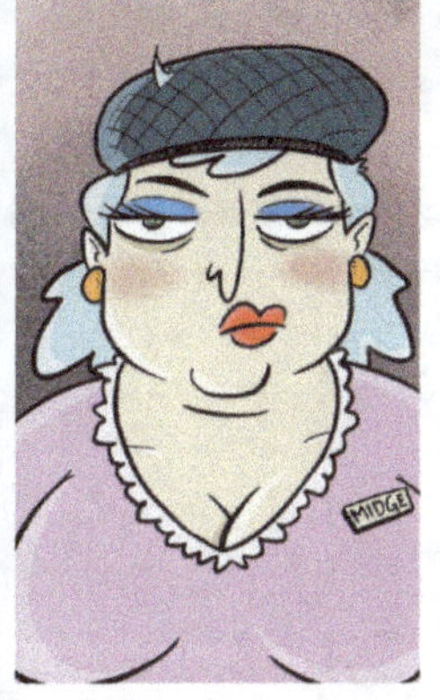

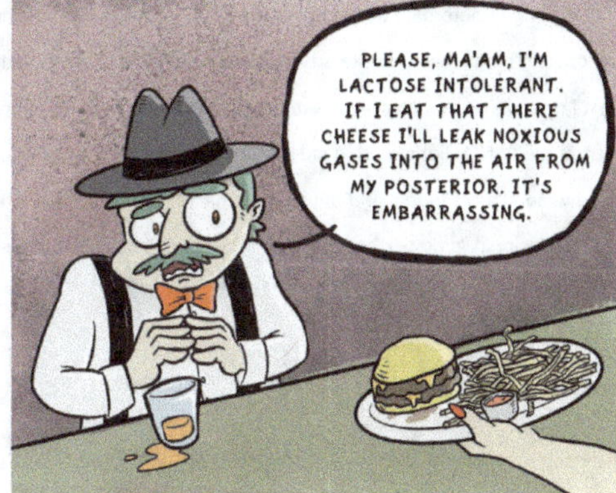

PLEASE, MA'AM, I'M LACTOSE INTOLERANT. IF I EAT THAT THERE CHEESE I'LL LEAK NOXIOUS GASES INTO THE AIR FROM MY POSTERIOR. IT'S EMBARRASSING.
MIDGE

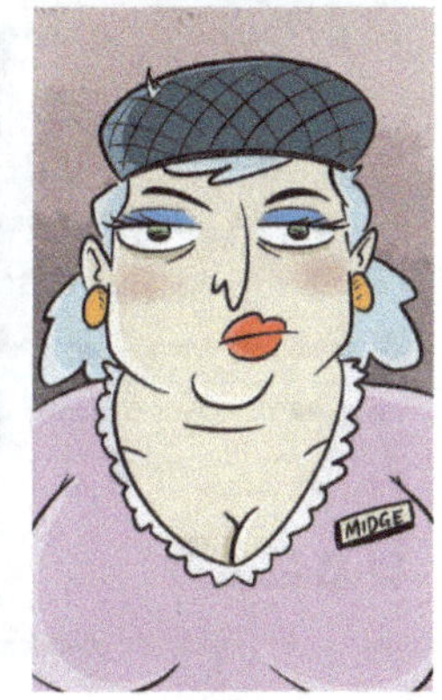

MIDGE

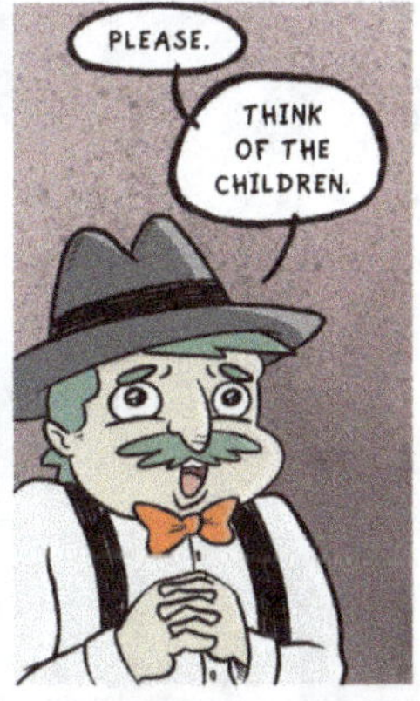

PLEASE.
THINK OF THE CHILDREN.

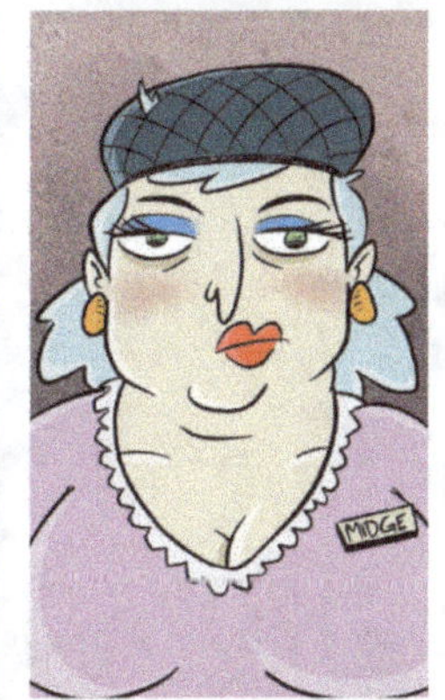

MIDGE

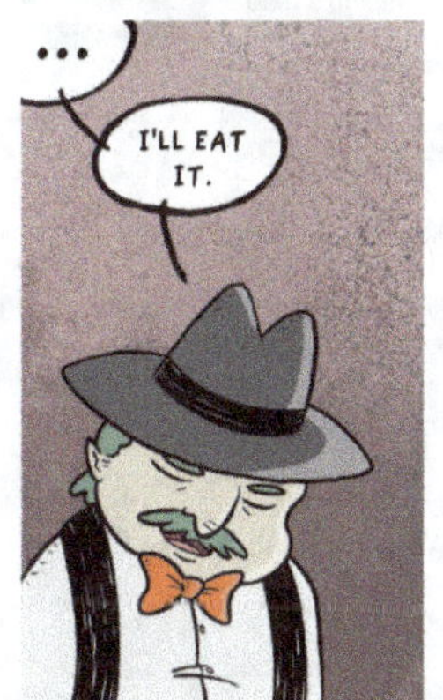

...
I'LL EAT IT.

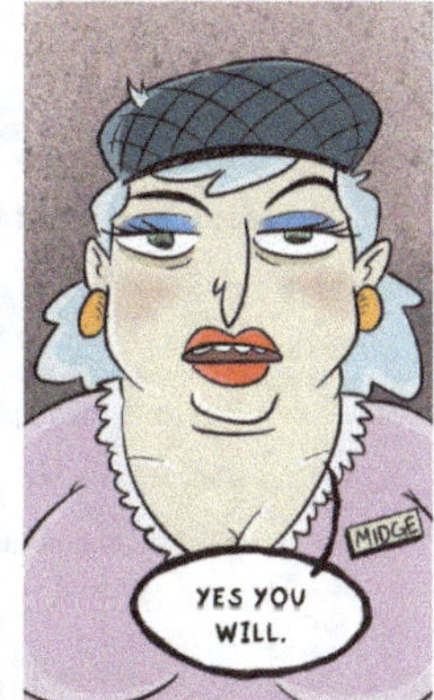

MIDGE
YES YOU WILL.

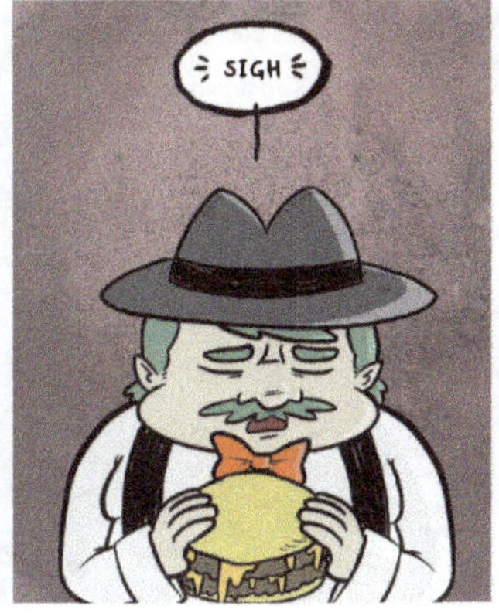

SIGH

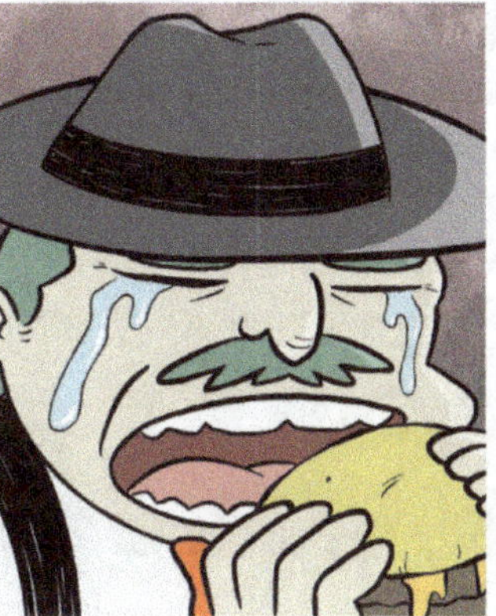

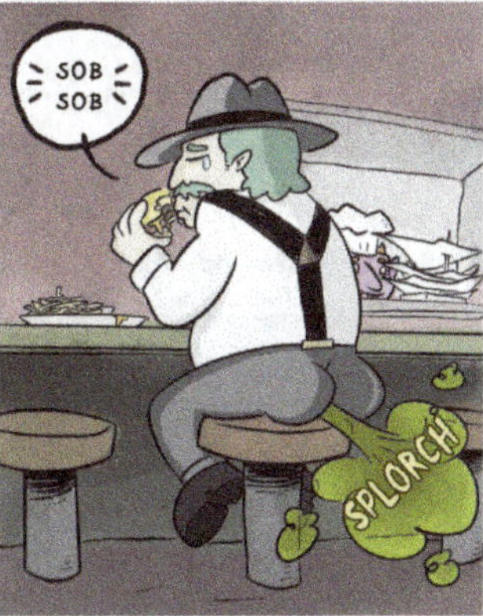

SOB SOB
SPLORCH!

Why?

Out of the gate – ND Riot does not pay its contributors. In this moment, this is a labor of love. Joe and Stephen share the editorial, financial, design, and other costs. Things that look like ads aren't; they're indie projects that deserve some attention. What we do offer is 1. A platform that hopefully shares your work with folks who love independent creatives. 2. Some long-term visibility. We're shooting to have every issue of ND Riot available at NDRiot.com soon. Since reviewing submissions takes time, we actually request a nominal $3 review fee. It's not much, and pays for the half-a-coffee Joe and Stephen will burn through while thoughtfully considering each submission. We do our best to respond within 14 days to submissions. All these realities are up for change as circumstance evolve.

What?

Mostly, we're looking for short-form comics, short stories, or other publishable creative work. While we will promote crowd-funded projects – our goal is to present something a reader

How?

Email the specific content you'd like featured to **Submissions@NDRiot.com**.

Here's what you should include:

- Your Name
- Website **or** one social media profile
- The content (minimum 300dpi)
- The $3 bribe sent to **Submissions@NDRiot.com** on PayPal.

www.ingramcontent.com/pod-product-compliance
Lightning Source LLC
Chambersburg PA
CBHW071231140726
47996CB00004B/1568

9798991806107